CHRISTOPHER J. STOCKWELL

Courting Mediocrity

Novella Two

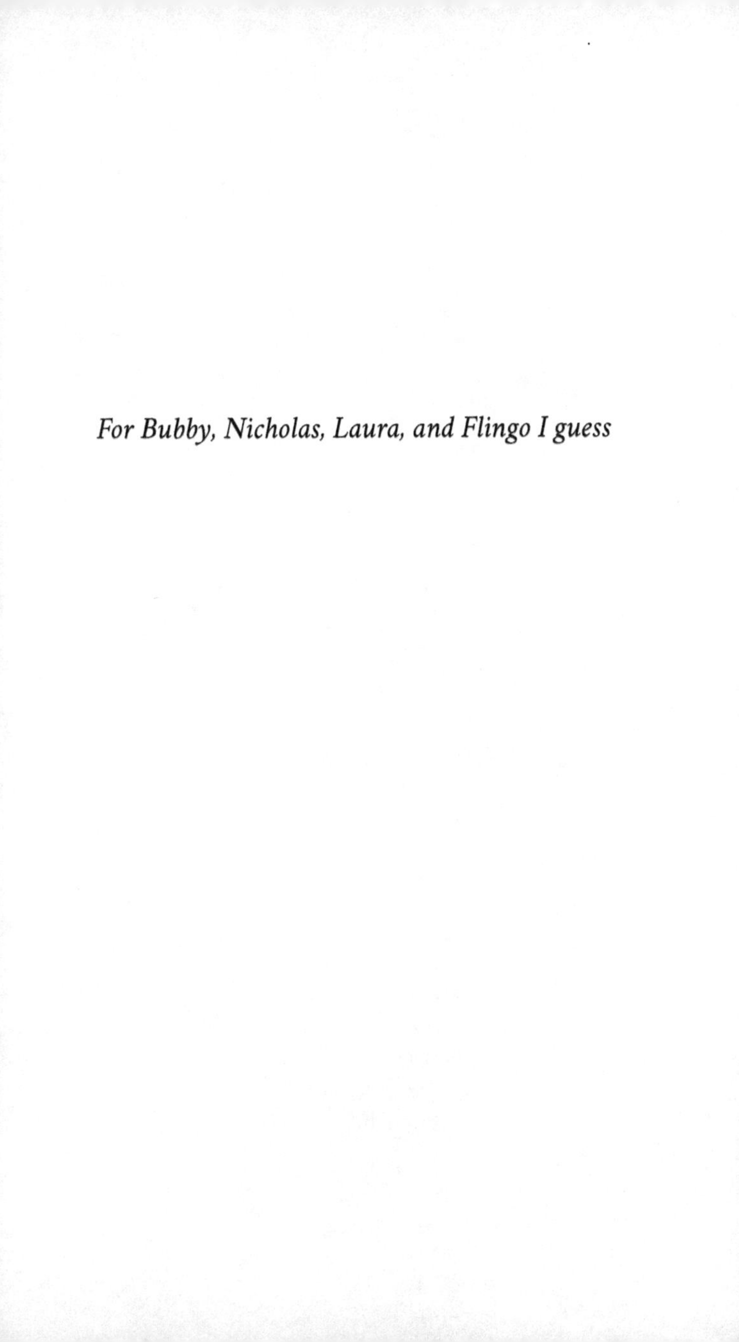

For Bubby, Nicholas, Laura, and Flingo I guess

Why do you insist upon destroying yourself?

—CHARLES BUKOWSKI,
HOLLYWOOD

Preface

"Why do you write?" She asked me during my first press interview for this book. "Why do you fuckin' care," is what my bestie Jack would say. He's always inside me trying to push his way out. When people take a tone, or give me orders, Jack bristles. Chris has a wife, kids, and a mortgage, so most of the time, Chris is charged with keeping Jack in check. Jack is why I write. The world moved on without Jack. His music scene is nothing but burnt ash from the campfire the night before. Jack's city doesn't exist anymore. It might as well be called Seattle 2.0.

I'm a lawyer, a prosecutor. When I put on a suit, you can't see me, or should I say you see my mask. Who am I? I'm the counterculture hiding in plain sight. Punk rock gave me a worldview, and I bring that worldview into society every time I speak in a courtroom or you flip the page of one of my books.

Why do I write, because after all these years, Jack and I are still pissed off at the world and everyone in it. And we've still got something to say about it.

Prologue

Was I speaking for Jack, or was Jack speaking for me? I'm the narrator, and while I do most of the speaking in this story, I never get an opportunity to really speak. Jack has got a lot to say, and most of it requires some high-brow interpretation from yours truly. The PNW hoi polloi vernacular takes a little gettin' used to, you know. Fortunately, I'm well versed. So well versed in fact, that it seems like Jack and I used to be the same person. If not the same, then nearly identical, and certainly inseparable.

At some point that changed. I'm not sure when, but it did. He went down the left fork, and I the right. Jack's story became more compelling as he became less salvageable. My story became less interesting as I became more capable. So I became the caretaker of Jack's story just as Beth became the caretaker of his mind. I hope I did it justice.

Chapter 1

One day, Beth had told Jack the strangest thing. The peehole belonged right at the tip of the head of the penis, not on the underside of the head. That put Jack's peephole clearly south of the mark. Like he needed something else to be paranoid about.

Jack's first trip to Western State Hospital had happened when he was eighteen. If Western State had taken juveniles, he would have ended up there sooner. Nobody could ever put their finger on exactly what Jack's mental problem had been, likely because he had suffered from so many mental disorders simultaneously. When he had arrived at Western State that first time, he had been transferred in an ambulance from Fairfax. Fairfax had had a juvenile facility for people like him. Nobody had known what was wrong with him at Fairfax, and nobody would figure it out at Western State either.

Among other things, Jack had been suffering a fairly nasty flare-up of his obsessive-compulsive disorder. At that time, it had been considered untreatable, and most had not thought of it as debilitating anyway. To most, even if they had been aware of it, OCD was just a personality quirk, not a severe mental illness. The more severe aspects of it, such as the accompanying anxiety, had been treated as discrete conditions, not symptoms of OCD.

In the ambulance, Jack had discovered a smell he had immediately named sanitized filth. An ambulance looked clean to a casual observer, just like a hospital did. Sanitized. But no place that saw as much filth and gore as an ambulance or hospital room could truly be clean. Every surface had seemed alive with it. It had danced on the defibrillator. It had snoozed in the suction device. It had leapt from one place to another on the net where the EMT's stethoscope had hung. The inside of that ambulance had been the most alive place Jack could ever remember having seen. That would have been entertaining if it hadn't been filth and disease animating the ambulance.

At that early stage of his mental illness, Jack would have found the thought of calling a place like Western State Hospital his home, even for a little while, repugnant. Just looking at the paramedic sitting on the bench seat next to him had put ideas into Jack's head about what he might be able to accomplish when that little stint of committal was over. Jack had thought he could fill that square-jawed EMT's uniform. He just needed to get his mind right, and then he would be off to EMT school.

In Jack's mind, he and the EMT hadn't been that different. They had both been about the same height and build, and they had even had a similar deviant look about them. But something in the EMT's life had steered him that way rather than this. He could just as easily have ended up a career criminal of some sort. In some other reality, he could have been the dope pusher, or even worse, the dope user. He could even have been the one lying on a gurney in an ambulance on his way to the funny farm. All had been possible options for the somewhat twisted-looking young man with the noble profession, but he had ended up there tending to Jack in the back of that ambulance. In Jack's opinion, all he had needed to do was recover a few of his marbles, and he could have had the guy's life within a year. Jack had been able to imagine a different life for himself like a champ. Unfortunately, imagining it had been about as far as he could usually get. Even imagining the different life had typically become boring to him after a few minutes.

Every few years, Jack had looked back over those that had just passed, and every time he had, he had always been left pondering one thought.

"Even with all the other things I could, or perhaps

should, be wonderin', or reflectin on, or tryin' to figure out, it's just that one thing that sticks with me. And that one thing is simply this: Whether those past few years have been good or bad didn't matter. What mattered is how I felt 'bout it those past few years. One thing that always comes to mind when I'm thinkin' 'bout those past few years is, if I had known what I'd be in for over the comin' years, if I would've just killed myself back then. Now I'm startin' to catch on. I'm pretty sure that in a few years I'll look back on this moment in time, and the years that came after, and wish that I'd killed myself today." Jack had delivered his message as cogently as he was capable.

"That sounds like bullshit to me, because if you felt good about the past few years, you wouldn't have wanted to kill yourself in retrospect. And whether they were good or bad must have some bearing on how you feel about them. I don't think you've ever had a good few years, and that, if you have no interest in changing, you never will. If the last few years were bad, then you should have plenty of motivation to do something different with the next few," Beth had said.

Beth had not suffered fools, and had tolerated little to no bullshit from Jack. She had always believed she was looking at a broken but fixable human being. This sappy pseudo-introspection had already become her least favorite part of Jack's personality, and she had intended to drum it out of him without delay.

"No, you don't really understand. If they'd been bad but productive, I'd feel differently. If I'd gotten somewhere, it would be different, but I haven't. And it seems like the next few years are going to just be more of the same," he had said.

"Well, maybe you're right, Jack. The next few years will likely be bad if you don't put recovery from your neuroses ahead of everything else. You've said a lot about how you sink into the shit, but I haven't heard anything about how you diligently apply yourself to changing your circumstances. Recovery from anything, whether it's purely a mental affliction or garden variety substance abuse, takes work. Can you work for recovery?"

That was the first time Jack had met Beth, and although he hadn't been sure that he was in love with her, he had been sure that he liked her better than anybody else in that place, and possibly anybody else on planet earth. Her mode of speaking to Jack had been direct and candid. Jack had never totally bought the rationalizations he had spun for the rest of the world. Most of his motivation had been to use the intelligence he was born with to justify his circumstances to others. Intellectualizing his poor circumstances was easier than dealing with them. Jack's ideal solution had been that this intellectualizing of his problems would somehow cause somebody to come along and fix his problems for him in one fell swoop. What Beth had advocated was taking action, and that had sounded like a lot of work to Jack. Jack had, characteristically, not been a huge fan of work.

"None of it really matters. What does matter is that I won't kill myself because I fear that Mormon doctrine on the subject may be true and I'll wind up in Hell, and guilt over what I'd be doing to my family keeps me from following through on it. Do you want to know what really bothers me, though?"

"You don't know how many more times in your life you'll be required to feel this way, and nobody, not even the best educated therapists, can give you any guarantee on your mental health. And you feel like the rest of your life is going to go as it has, just one empty, miserable year after another, like doing time in a penitentiary. Were you going to tell me something like that?" Beth said.

She had said it as though it had been said to her many times before. Jack had hit a bit of a roadblock. Beth hadn't been mean to him, so he hadn't been able to write her off as just some cold bitch. She hadn't bought his narrative, and she had simultaneously challenged him to be better. Normally, this was where Jack would have found some way to put some distance between himself and her. And if you had known Jack, this would have made all the sense in the world. As mentioned, one thing Jack had always despised was work. He had wanted to be around this Beth person, but she had wanted him to attempt to improve his circumstances by doing uncomfortable things. He really hadn't known what to do with that. For whatever reason, at that time, and for that one person, he had wanted to be better.

Beth was twenty-three and just months out of nursing school when they had met. She had been an LPN. LPN was the nursing course of choice for people whose ambitions, funding, or attention spans would only allow a year's schooling. Even the name sounded lame. *Licensed practical nurse.* It was like you were practically a nurse—not actually, but practically.

Beth had been a different story, though. Most bright and ambitious people that wanted to go into nursing found a way to complete an RN program. They then became productive members of the middle class with good jobs. Someday, that would be Beth, but back then she had just been a green LPN recently out of an abusive and short-lived marriage. Jack had imagined that marriage was what kept her from finding a career until then. The truth was more interesting than he had imagined.

Beth had gone just awry of normal and had spent

her teens and early twenties developing addictions to a variety of prescription pain medications and alcohol. After the end of a brief and miserable marriage, and a short stint at an inpatient drug and alcohol rehab program, she'd decided that nursing was the career she wanted to pursue. She had been a fuck-up half-breed. Jack, on the other hand, had been a fuck-up pure-breed. So of course, Beth had spoken Jack's language better than some overeducated therapist ever could have. However, unlike all the other fuckups in Jack's life, Beth's words had carried credence. Remember, she had been a fuckup half-breed. She had walked in two worlds simultaneously, so the stories she had brought from the normal world were practical and believable.

Even though he was pretty new at the whole institution circuit, Jack had already begun to notice some similarities they all shared. Actually, he had noticed that most things from institution to institution were very similar. People were different, just as locations were different; even the methods in which various facilities were funded were different. But really, they were all the same. The people at Western State had really just been replicas of their Fairfax counterparts. Just as the interior layout and outside grounds had just been copies of copies of still other copies of some master planned institution conceived in some architect's mind and residing outside a sleepy New England town.

In a future Jack could only imagine, he was a millionaire. He'd developed a PC game that was a simulation of institutional living. Years of institutional living had uniquely qualified him to create such an unquestionably controversial game. It was a true simulation, 3D graphics and all, everything you'd ever need to know to survive in an institutional setting, and more.

Cheeking your meds at the nurse's station so you could trade them or dope up on them later when you'd saved enough to get really high would be a Level One skill. Level One was behavioral and mental institutions.

The Level Two series of simulations would bring you through the gauntlet known as substance abuse institutions, halfway houses, and homeless shelters.

And, finally, there would be the most fearsome of simulations: the criminal justice system that brought you through the journey from arrest right into the county tank or city jail, followed by your trial, and finally the state penitentiary. Of course, your crimes would determine whether you went to a minimum, medium, or maximum-security prison. Upon arrival, your behavior would determine which gangs would be interested in you as a potential member or target.

The caption "Good luck" would be emblazoned on the front of the game box, along with graphic animations of some of the nastier aspects of institution life, informing the potential buyer of the violent nature of the game. In Jack's mind, he figured it would be so mature and violent in nature that they'd have to invent some parental advisory label for it, sort of like the ones they started putting on all the punk, rap, and metal records a couple of years before. He had laughed to himself. "Like they'd ever put warnin' labels on fuckin' video games! Movies and records, sure, but a video game, no fuckin' way."

Nintendo would buy the game outright and develop a version for their game console. It would look great, like 3D Worldrunner in institutions. The best thing was that it would be a true hybrid between a first-person action and role-playing game.

"Somehow, my poor luck, bent mind, and painful life experiences had paid off to the tune of millions. It seemed too good to be true, and there was just one thing that could make life sweeter. It was finally my opportunity to rub Laurence's face in my fuckin' success, and I'd do it by givin' him a few hundred thousand bucks. There couldn't be anythin' more humiliatin' for Laurence, but he would have no choice but to accept. And every time he looked at whatever he bought with the money he'd re-live that humiliation. Just as ultimate revenge for my wasted life was within my grasp, I awoke to the sound of a ten-pound sledgehammer fist beating on the door to my room. It was Jon, the orderly. He was a huge man, and he was there to hold me down while a nurse administered my Thorazine shot. Good fuckin' times."

The first ones that you noticed were the droolers. They stuck out. When you thought about a ward in a mental hospital, the droolers were the first ones that came to mind. There was that scene at the end of *One Flew Over the Cuckoo's Nest*, where McMurphy comes back from his lobotomy. Nobody's home. Yeah, they made him a drooler. Droolers didn't like to stay in their rooms, either. Something about drooling all over the common areas really made their worlds go around. You could almost see their tiny, expressionless faces light up when you went to lean on a handrail and your hand landed in a big, gooey pile of saliva. Even more fun than that was when someone fell right down a set of steps because the pool of handrail saliva they'd put their hand in was really slippery. Of course, they were mostly just walking shells of humans, but with a little imagination you could tell a few things were still going on in their blank little minds. Besides, after receiving icepicks to the brain, they deserved a little comedy in their lives. Not that lobotomies had still taken place by the time Jack had made the institution circuit. Still, some of them had been so old, they might have been the recipients of the icepick back in the day. Although Jack imagined most of them had wound up that way naturally, or that it had been brought on by the drugs they received for decades there at Western State.

The wall walkers had stuck out too, and Jack had really had a soft spot for them. By virtue of being in the hallways all the time, they were usually the next ones that you ran into. "It just makes sense, if you think 'bout it. I mean, if you're hangin' around in the common areas, you're going to get seen. It's like a runway at a fashion show. Everybody else is just sitting in a folding chair, but all eyes were on the droolers and wall walkers." By the same Jack logic, they had also been the ones that most commonly stuck their hands in the drool on the handrails. "Come on, I mean, they're literally leanin' on the walls when they're walkin', of course they're going to get the handrail saliva. Watchin' a wall walker take a header after grabbin' handrail saliva, that's good times for everyone involved, except for the wall walkers I guess. When their hands slide off the handrails, and they lose their footin' on the linoleum, a nasty spill was sure to follow. There is no greater joy in the mental ward than an especially active afternoon of watchin' wall walkers givin themselves serious head trauma after slippin' and slidin' in the droolers' saliva pools. If I had a video camera in here, I'd sell the videos on late night TV. I'd be a fuckin' millionaire."

On one such afternoon, Jack had sat at a table in the common room of C-Ward. There had been a checkerboard in front of him with the remnants of a red checker victory still on it. He had wished there was a chess board in the ward, but he had immediately realized even if there was, there probably wouldn't have been anybody on C-Ward with enough of their marbles left to actually play. With all the Thorazine, Jack had doubted he could even play the game worth a shit himself. Right then, he had witnessed a wall walker take an epic header. He had known it was handrail saliva. Jack had just seen Mary, one of the more active droolers, over by that stairwell a few minutes ago. She'd made a quick escape in her wheelchair when she had noticed Jack looking over at her. That had been where the epiphany happened. Wall walkers that took epic headers sometimes suffered severe head trauma, enough head trauma to turn them into droolers. "That's how the fuckin' droolers were reproducin'." Jack had never touched a handrail at Western State again. "I got my fuckin' issues, but I ain't ready to be a fuckin' drooler. I walk up and down them steps with my arms crossed. It looks weird when I do it, but shit, you just do what you got to do to get by, you know."

Jack had also asked for a notebook and a pen. He had spent the next three days obsessively writing a horror movie screenplay about the droolers' slow-moving plan to take over Western State through handrail drool headers. Jack had been the main character, and the genius that ultimately foiled the droolers' plan of taking over Western State. At least he would have been, but Jack had gotten bored of the screenplay right around the time he had developed the hivemind aspect of the droolers' existence. As with most of Jack's great ideas, the screenplay had been better used as a hook that had allowed him to daydream about making it big someday. When Jack had left Western State, he had packed the spiral notebook containing his unfinished screenplay, *The Droolers*, into a box. That box had gone into a storage closet at his mom's house, and years later it had gone right into the garbage when Laurence had cleaned out their mom's house after she had died. Even Jack had to recognize that there was no maliciousness on Laurence's part here. It had been a box labeled "Jack's stuff from Western State." When deciding what to do with all the things in his dead mom's home, Jack's stuff from Western State had seemed like an obvious choice for the dumpster. The sad part was, *The Droolers* had actually been good, and in other circumstances, a guy like Jack probably could have made a living writing screenplays for low-budget horror movies.

Other than walking with the sides of their faces and torsos glued to the walls, the wall walkers had mostly been uninteresting to the people at Western State. All they had really done was walk along walls and moan. Nonetheless, Jack had been endlessly fascinated by them. He had decided that if *The Droolers* got made into a movie, he'd write a sequel and call it *The Wall Walkers*. He had liked the wall walkers so much that he had felt bad they would only get the sequel, but even he'd had to realize that droolers, with their hivemind and unconventional method of reproducing, were pure movie gold, whereas wall walkers were pretty one-dimensional.

It was the difference between vampires and zombies. While Jack had loved zombies, they didn't really do much. Vampires, however, were complex and interesting. Anyway, as far as low-budget horror movies were concerned, droolers had clearly needed to come first, even if Jack had ultimately preferred wall walkers.

On the subject of moaning, there had always been a few of those, too. Moaners hadn't really constituted a class of their own, though. The main reason was that sometimes wall walkers had moaned, and sometimes even droolers had moaned. Even Cliff Clavins had moaned when they were jacked on Thorazine. For that matter, Jack had moaned sometimes for various reasons, including the Thorazine. Sometimes he had thought the employees were going to start moaning. Every once in a while, you would get some weirdo who only lay in their bed and moaned. This rare breed, a pure moaner, had been the exception, and the only kind of person that could really lay claim to the title "moaner." Plus, they had been even simpler than wall walkers. At least wall walkers had roamed around. Pure moaners had just laid in bed. Therefore, Jack had refused to characterize them as a discreet group of their own.

If you made it to the TV room, you'd have been bound to run into a few of the aforementioned Cliff Clavins. The Cliff Clavins had always been in the TV room, always coming up with new conspiracy theories. The local news had been good for getting them going, and the national evening news had been even better, but the good Cliff Clavins had been able to get a conspiracy theory going about a twenty-year-old sitcom. Jack had even heard some good ones during Saturday morning cartoons. Newspapers had also been a rich source of conspiracy material for the overactive, mentally impaired minds. Most of the Cliff Clavins' conspiracies had focused on the government taking control of your mind through media or locking people up for trying to expose their master plans for mind-control of citizens in the name of global domination. Since they had all actually been locked up by the government, some of their conspiracy theories had almost made sense to Jack, but then something like alien overlords had always arrived in the narrative, and Jack had remembered he was in a mental hospital. The particulars of the day's conspiracy theory hadn't really mattered. The themes were always the same, but listening to a Cliff Clavin explain a conspiracy theory in detail had been a good way to kill time. You had at least been able to have a conversation with a Cliff Clavin, unlike most of the residents of C-Ward.

Screamers had been mostly boring and loud. Those screams had cut through Jack's skin the way a sharp knife sliced through your finger when you missed while cutting an onion. Then nothing—no explanation, no context, just screams—then quiet. At least the wall walkers had done interesting things like fondle the walls in inappropriate ways. Between their skin-slicing screams, the mystery stemming from lack of interesting backstories for said screams, and the fact that they could agitate staff as well as patients, they had qualified as a group worthy of an official title. They had definitely been irritating, but they had been a discrete group worthy of an official title, just barely.

The last major category of patient you normally ran into in a mental ward was the impersonator, or helper. The terms were mostly interchangeable. Sometimes, a patient had just been a helper, or had just been an impersonator, but if a person was one, they were probably both. Depending on who was around, you could have been talking to the impersonator, or the helper. When hospital staff was present, you were probably dealing with the helper. This person had kissed the staffs' asses when they are around. When staff hadn't been around, they had pretended to be members of the staff when family members had come to visit or EMS crews had dropped off new patients. They had even tried to fool new patients and hospital staff from other areas of the hospital. Sometimes they had been pretty good at it, too.

"I've seen paramedics give entire reports on in-comin' patients to an impersonator. Meds, history, chief complaint, the whole ball of wax, then an LPN walks up and sends the impersonator to the day room. As a professional, that's got to be fuckin' embarrassin'. But it's understandable; most of the staff didn't wear any visible identification. Plus, most of them wore street clothes. The nurses wore scrubs, but impersonators would get into the storage room where the scrubs were kept. They would put them on and walk around the ward all the fuckin' time. It doesn't help that when a patient is brought in off the street, and their clothes needed to be washed, that hospital staff put them in scrubs. Always look down in a mental ward. This is a hard and fast rule that will allow you to always know if you are talkin to an impersonator. Patients don't have shoelaces, ever. Even though I knew everybody that worked on C-Ward, I still looked down before I took my meds from them. Never swallow unless you see the shoelaces of the nurse giving you the meds. Who knows what some of the psychos around there would try to stick in your med cup."

There had been some positive things about the C-Ward, and all the facilities like it. That one in particular had allowed Jack to eat basically however much he liked. The wall walkers and droolers had barely eaten anything, but they had been given full meals just like the rest of the patients. They had never seemed to complain when Jack had grabbed the meal of a patient that was neglecting it. He hadn't just stolen their food. He had always made sure that they weren't going to eat it first. But he had figured, why waste good food? If Jack hadn't eaten their food, it had just gone into the garbage. Sometimes, getting an extra dessert hadn't been worth it, though. Getting food from a drooler second-hand hadn't typically been a great plan. If it had been in their possession for more than about thirty seconds it had gotten drool on it. That was a lesson Jack had learned the hard way more than once. Jack had even tried wiping drool off food he really wanted—or, if it was soup, just stirring the drool in. After doing this ten or twelve times, he had learned that sometimes it was better to just let it go in the garbage can. Wall walker food had been great, though—always nice and dry.

Not only that, but he had been left alone to do his own thing most of the time. "If a guy weren't careful, he might even be able to get his head together in a place like this." Jack had known it wasn't going to happen by going to group, or taking his meds, but by just having time to reflect on what had gone wrong and determine how to rectify the things in the past that pertained to the future. He had imagined driving down avenues of refrain, cruising effortlessly past those things that had brought him down once on the outside. And that was what Jack had done with most of his time.

Following the program had been for losers, or for the lifers that would never leave there. Jack had known it. He wasn't normal, but he had teetered a lot closer to it than the freaks there on C-Ward. In his mind, that had given him the right to skip group or meetings with the psychiatrist. It had given him the right to sit in his room and read or spend time with Beth. When the RN on the ward had made Beth go back to work and stop wasting time with Jack, he had gone to the dayroom and monopolized the TV. He hadn't partially inhabited normalcy like Beth had, but his nearness to normalcy had entitled him to play TV remote dictator and occasionally, when one of the Cliff Clavins wouldn't shut up, boot their ass out of the room all together.

Jack had been young, strong, and, as mentioned, in a proximity to sanity that had made him a mental god compared to the other patients there. Also, he had had a girlfriend, and that girlfriend had access to drugs. So, basically, Jack had been the kingpin of C-Ward, and before long the Cliff Clavins had even made-up conspiracy theories about him. In one of them, Jack hadn't even been a patient; he was an agent of the State of Washington. The place being a state-owned and run facility had made the whole mole-for-the-state theory work for the rat in a maze line of thinking that was the predominate thought process of most of the residents there. That is, the ones capable of thinking at all. The fact that his girlfriend had happened to be one of their nurses had only added fuel to the fire. Soon enough, the Cliff Clavins and everybody else had just left the dayroom when Jack had wanted to watch TV. Nobody would bunk in the same room with him, so he had been moved into a single room. It was smaller, but he'd had it all to himself.

In a strange way, he had stayed off the staff's radar by being the guy nobody wanted to talk to. In any real rehabilitative setting, he wouldn't have been able to intimidate people into letting him do what he pleased whenever he wanted. In a real rehabilitative setting, the staff would have cared about trying to actually help people assimilate back into society. Instead, the staff there had only seemed to truly care about keeping the patients doped up enough that they were docile twenty-four hours a day. There had been no real treatment with medication there. People hadn't been medicated to treat their affliction. They had been medicated for how they acted. Act badly, and you were medicated heavily. Intimidate patients and keep to yourself, you were left to set your own agenda, just so long as you didn't do anything that gave the staff headaches. For Jack, that had included which meds he'd take. Once Jack had been able to dictate what would and wouldn't go into his body the Thorazine had stopped for good. "Too much of that stuff too often will turn you right into a fuckin' drooler, and like I already said, I had zero plans on becomin a drooler."

Dr. Snyder had become interested in Jack's situation right around the time he'd resolved himself to just staying at Western State forever. Much like many inmates and patients that had come before,

Jack had embraced making Western State home. The inside had become better than the outside for Jack. Plus, he hadn't even really known how to get along on the outside, anyway, so this seemed like a no-brainer to him. He had been institutionalized. Unlike many inmates and patients in lockdowns and hospitals throughout the world, Jack had had things especially good. What more could he have asked for? He'd had a girl, any variety of drugs at his disposal, and an army of patients who he had been able to dominate. The patients hadn't liked him, but they hadn't challenged him either.

In the good doctor's opinion, anybody who was able to dominate an entire mental ward was more than ready to leave that ward and go live on the outside. It had been a strange position to be in for Jack. After all, in all his life, he'd never been a victim of his own success, and now he'd have to leave his home because of his uncanny ability to thrive in that environment. In the background, the doctor's voice had pedantically rambled on about keeping his weekly appointments with his state-appointed therapist and, of course, staying on the med program that she'd lay out for Jack. Most important, she had said, would be for Jack to find a positive outlet for his otherwise-criminally-minded behavior. In his head, what he had gotten out of this conversation was that his physician had called him gifted, albeit only at corrupt endeavors. Also, that his sharp, self-centered mind was the reason he had been released. The other thing that had become clear to Jack was that no matter how well he'd been able to manipulate the patients of C-Ward, he was a failure when it came to fooling the doctors. And for that reason, Jack had been expelled from his home. The next time, he had resolved to manage better.

Chapter 2

"You know what I had plenty of time to ponder during those months of confinement? Why are there these gill lookin' things on both sides of the head of my cock? These things are right under this weird flap of skin, and there's always this pasty white stuff by them. Wait, don't tell me that's some more abnormal penis shit, too. Whatever."

Jack had spent nine months confined at Western State. Freshly nineteen, and freshly back on the street, he had decided to make a fresh start. Nine months had been plenty of time for Jack's mom to save up some starting-out money for him. His mom had stashed thirty-five hundred dollars away in an account, just waiting to help Jack get back on his feet. That had just been the living expense money. If he had become interested in higher education, there was a college fund at her disposal with his name on it, too.

Although his parents hadn't been rich, they had always been financially capable of taking care of

Laurence and Jack. Jack had always believed his mom wanted a couple more children. Jack was sure his father had refused on the grounds that they could really only afford to provide properly for the two they'd already had. Flawed logic, to say the least. Even Jack knew that the more kids you had, the cheaper they got to raise. Bulk meals, hand-me-downs, shared bedrooms. "Shit, if you have enough of 'em, you probably start breakin' even financially. If you have enough of 'em they may even turn into a money-making enterprise at some point. Just look at the Osmonds, or the Jacksons, the fuckin' Partridge Family. I know that last one is just on TV, but still."

Lacking quantity of children had forced Jack's mom to the other extreme. That is, spoiling the two she *had* had. Regrettably for his mom, college hadn't been on Jack's radar screen, and neither had a job.

What *had* been on Jack's radar screen? Debauchery naturally. Debauchery and, of course, any flavor of lawlessness that might have elevated Jack to the stratosphere of leadership and power in the real world that he'd enjoyed at Western State. Those heights of success that he had envisioned for himself had always seemed to elude him. When he thought about it, he could never say for certain what should have happened to make it turn out right.

Sometimes, it seemed to him that his wasted life

had been spent in hollow pursuits. Sometimes, it seemed that his wasted life never could have turned out to be anything other than what it had become.

When Jack looked at other people with their seemingly normal lives, Jack wondered if he had ever even possessed the capacity to become educated, employed, and otherwise entrapped into ignorance and middle-class bliss. His conclusion had always been *probably not*, so he figured he should become whatever variety of criminal would allow him to still get normal people's creature comforts. "I think it's the condo. I really want the condo in the city. Those are my favorite daydreams of the future, the ones where I am a heroin-dealin' kingpin. In those daydreams, I always have the condo in the city.

Everybody had to start somewhere. Jack had started in a two-bedroom house in a small neighborhood just outside of Tacoma called Parkland. The biggest thing going on in Parkland in the late eighties had been the college campus. And there had been an old twin theater called The Parkland Theater. "I know, real fuckin' original name. At least the theater was more interestin' than the Walgreens they built there after they demolished it."

The college, Pacific Lutheran University, had been the most expensive, most private, most religious, and most exclusive college in the state. Jack had set up shop two blocks away. College kids needed drugs, that was just common sense, and Jack had been there to provide. Even though he had only been nineteen, and barely that, in life experience he was already light years ahead of those college kids. They had been getting their education. Jack had already had all the education he'd ever need to do what he did.

Jack's clothes, his '81 Volvo, and his rathole two-bedroom house two blocks from the college campus had all been signals to the rest of the world that he was a spoiled college kid whose parents had footed the bill for his life from tuition to toilet paper. Of course, that was what it had all said; that was what it was supposed to say. Jack's backpack had even had textbooks in it. They had sat right on top of the hidden pouch he'd sewn into the bottom of it. The pouch, of course, had held Jack's mobile stash, as well as his easily concealable Walther PPK. Some sophomore kid had needed more blow to get through midterms than he could swing on his allowance. That kid had needed the blow, and Jack had needed a gun. The kid's dad had needed the kid to pass his classes so that he could become some prick lawyer like daddy. His dad certainly hadn't missed that pistol. Besides, a Walther PPK? That was James Bond's gun. how could Jack have passed on that?

Out of his little home, he dealt everything—

everything there had been a market for, that is. Jack had a pager before anyone else he had known. He was the only person he had known who had routinely carried hundred-dollar bills in wads that added up to thousands. And he was the only person he knew that had carried a loaded gun. It was Washington State, rainforests as far as the eye could see in every direction, so everybody had owned a hunting rifle. The dealers on Hilltop in Tacoma had carried loaded pistols, but out there in Parkland in the eighties, a dealer with a loaded pistol had been an aberration.

The beauty of the upscale college campus had been that as long you were one of them, and you didn't rock the boat, they had let much slide. In their eyes, Jack had been one of them. At first, he had just hung around campus, gone to parties and sporting events—shit like that. That had been how he first built up his clientele. But, after a while, he had wanted more access to the campus. If you strolled around campus long, and often enough, Campus Safety (which was what PLU called their security people) would eventually start asking you questions. That would have been fine if you happened to be your garden-variety loiterer, but Jack had been packing a Walther, a pager, a couple grand in cash, and an ass-load of illegal substances that could have netted him some real time in the tank. Jack had known it was time to dummy up a fake student ID.

In those days, getting a fake college ID had been pretty easy. At the game room in the student center, people had used their student IDs to rent pool tables. The little rack the game room staff had kept the IDs on was easily reachable from the other side of the counter. One day, Jack had just reached over and grabbed a student ID when the person minding the counter had been tending to something on the other side of the game room. He had taken a razor blade and cut the picture off, taken a picture of himself that matched the gray backdrop of the ID's original photo, glued it on, cut the extra lamination from the margins, and had it re-laminated at Kinkos. In the end, most of it had been double-laminated, but it hadn't looked suspect, and Jack had used it numerous times around campus to prove his enrolled student status.

Jack had had numerous close calls around campus, but they hadn't scared him off. Campus safety had literally caught him in the middle of a deal by the bike rack outside the library on campus. Even though the security guy had known what was going on, he had been too far away to say for sure, and he hadn't even tried to detain Jack and his buyer. He had asked for both of their student IDs and told Jack to stop dealing on campus. Jack hadn't minded close calls. He had just adopted new techniques for dealing with them. That security guy had looked at Jack's fake ID for a little too long for Jack's comfort, and after that Jack had known it was time to step up his game.

Being able to pass as a student had helped out a lot in the beginning, but really being a student, at least on paper, was the next step. One of Jack's best customers had done his work-study in the admissions office. This client had been more than happy to set Jack up as a student in the college system for a few ounces of chronic. "Who knew that becomin' a student was just a matter of shufflin' some papers around and enterin' some crap info into a computer. Crazy, huh!" This customer had had access to a computer platform that had allowed him to make a student file for Jack, and it had even been under his own name. For all intents and purposes, Jack had been a student at PLU. His electronic student file had been pretty spartan, so if anybody had dug too deeply into his file, they'd have noticed that he had no grades, was enrolled in no classes, and had never even filled out a college application. But he was in the system, so he had been able to go get a real college ID card from the office that issued them. For the casual run-ins with Campus Safety, or faculty, it had worked perfectly. His sparse student profile had never been questioned or even looked into, so far as Jack knew.

During that time, Jack actually had gotten a bit of an education. Because he had been on campus all the time, and because he had been constantly trying to expand his customer base, he had started looking at the semester class schedules. He had picked a few classes that sounded interesting to him, things like political science, economics, some history classes. Then he had started actually attending them. He had only gone to classes that had large enrollments, and that met in the big lecture halls. That way, nobody ever called on him, or even inquired as to what he was doing there. He had been just another anonymous face in a freshman course with a hundred other anonymous faces.

Jack had noticed, with some disappointment, that he couldn't really sit in the upper-level classes of the subjects he liked. Those courses had been smaller, and he had not been able to blend into the background so easily. "Sure, a hundred people will sign up to take the freshman level political science course, but only political science majors would enroll for a class called America's Role in Nation Building after World War II. Oh fuckin' well! Too bad, I really thought that one sounded interestin'." A few times, he had been able to blend in a class of forty or fifty, but even that had been a stretch. He had even gotten the books and done the readings for those smaller classes so that he could talk in class if he was called on and participate in class activities like small group discussions.

Jack had felt pretty good about himself. Six months out of Western State, and he hadn't been able to see anything horrible on the horizon. His little home had been the roughest-looking thing on the block of 119th Street and Park Avenue South. Jack's house had been such an eyesore that many people on the block had thought it was abandoned. One day, two kids, eleven or twelve-year-old boys, had ridden by when Jack was checking his mail. The bigger one had said, "I didn't know you could get mail at abandoned houses." After some inquiry from Jack, he had learned that this kid's parents, and apparently numerous people on the block, referred to his house as the "abandoned house," so after Jack had told the story to a few people, the name had sort of stuck.

It hadn't been an unfair characterization. The house hadn't had a lawn so much as it had had scattered random patches of brownish grass accompanied by green weeds and dandelions. Jack had never really thought about how the yard looked, and he certainly hadn't given a crap about grass. After talking to those kids, he had taken his first real hard look at the yard, and he had started to see what their parents had. Also, there had been no driveway, just tire tracks through the part of the yard closest to the front door. That was where Jack had parked. He had called it the driveway. Everybody else had parked in the actual yard. Quite to Jack's amusement, he had just noticed for the first time a horribly rusted lawnmower being strangled by interwoven blackberry vines sitting in the corner of the yard next to an equally rusted, prefabbed metal shed. It was not lost on him that the last time someone had bothered to mow the yard, that mower had probably been used to do it.

The yard was a suburbanite's worst nightmare from top to bottom, and there had even been a tire on its side, full of dirt, near the living room window housing the remains of some poorly neglected plant. This had clearly been some prior resident's attempt to grow something using the tire as a planter. Knowing the types of people likely to rent a place like that, Jack had had a pretty good idea of what they had been growing. That said, the house itself had been no better. It had been about four different colors. Jack's best guess was that whoever had built the sad little shack had been trying to save money and decided to only buy a little paint at a time, hoping that the next bucket would finish the job. When it hadn't, he'd run back to the store, and they hadn't been able to mix the paint to an exact match. Voila, a four-color house. There had been cables hanging off it, running to the street or to a box on the side of the house. Jack doubted most of those cables had done anything, and had probably just been remnants of a bygone cable TV installation, or re-routing of a phone line extension. The roof shingles had hung on by single nails and draped themselves over algae-stained gutters like they had been some sort of economically challenged style accent.

As terrible as the outside was, the inside had actually been pretty clean. Nobody would have called it cozy, with its standard white paint throughout and cheap gray carpet. Between the white walls and gray carpet, the house had always seemed a little chilly, sort of like being in the tundra. The appliances had been well past their prime, but at least they had been clean. Jack had supposed the oven was from the fifties. Before he had moved in, cleaners had soaked the bowl-shaped metal things that went under the burners and used some Easy Off on the inside. The refrigerator was similarly ancient, but the landlord had made some effort to clean it out properly. The freezer had even been defrosted when Jack had first gotten there.

The linoleum tiles had looked like kaleidoscopes with oddly colored filigree patterns flanking them. It had been dingy but mostly unnoticeable, unless you moved an appliance. Jack hadn't even known the background on the linoleum was supposed to be white until he had moved the refrigerator one time. Nor had he noticed how spongy that flooring had been until he had seen where the wheels of the refrigerator had sunk a quarter of an inch into that linoleum. When he had rolled the refrigerator back, the wheels had dropped into their little burrows like a revolver's cylinder clicking into place.

Other high points of the house: Jack's room had had a plywood door, like it was some sort of kid's fort, or a kitchen cabinet. There hadn't even been a doorknob, just a janky hook and loop to keep his door closed. The spare room had had no door at all, just a frame with the frame portion of the door hinges still attached. Strangest of all, the bathroom had been carpeted with the same cheap gray carpet that ran throughout the living and bedrooms. This hadn't been a problem at first, but a few months of Jack and Todd drunkenly missing the bowl while peeing had made it a problem. The smell had become overpowering, and their many efforts to mitigate it by spraying carpet cleaner all over it had proven to be futile. In fact, the mix of the cleaner and urine together had quite possibly been worse than the urine alone.

It was so early on in Jack's story that the core of his crew had been intact, and more or less working together. Todd hadn't really been working, but he was around. He had been around, smoking, slamming, dropping, and swallowing every substance that Jack had managed to sling on a regular basis. Todd had been pulling a paycheck from somewhere for doing nothing, like usual. Mostly he had been living in the spare bedroom at the abandoned house. That had been fine with Jack. That had just meant that Jack hadn't needed to quality-test every shipment of product that he had bought in quantity. Todd had been a more than willing guinea pig. Having to be stoned out of his mind when he was trying to buy drugs was a real hinderance to Jack anyway, and after Todd moved in, he hadn't needed to be. Also, it had meant that there was always somebody around the house to keep an eye on things. Jack had owned a decent Sentry safe, but that wouldn't have stopped somebody from just walking off with it if nobody had been around. Jack was pessimistic and had preferred to err on the side of extreme paranoia, even when it was just for suspicion's sake. Regardless, having Todd sitting there all day while Jack was out about his business had been a pretty huge benefit to him.

Because Todd had been there all the time, Jack had mostly stopped worrying about being robbed. Besides, Parkland had been a small town, and the PLU campus had been even smaller, and Jack had figured that if he ever did get robbed, it wouldn't have taken him long to figure out who had done it. Anyway, with Todd, who seldom left the couch, sitting there lit up all day long, the chances had been good that he'd have blown you away with that .357 Magnum cannon he called a gun. He had almost cut Jack in half with that thing half a dozen times coming through the front door, which was also the back door, or in other words the only door. That was one of the things Jack had liked best about this house: one way in, one way out. That one way out had had two bullet holes in the door jamb. One day, Todd had been doing lines of crank all afternoon and watching *Taxi Driver*. Next thing you know, Jack had come strolling through the door, a day early from a camping trip, and Todd had gone all Travis Bickle. Luckily for Jack, Todd had not been as good a shot as Travis. After that, Jack had told Todd either no more crank for him, or no more loaded .357 Magnum in the house. He had laid off the crank for a while, but the .357 Magnum had stayed loaded.

Mike had been doing the whole having a job and girlfriend thing. It seemed like every few years people had to endure this phase of life. People like Jack were well-versed in this type of relationship. You met a girl, she went out with you despite the fact that you had nothing going on, and after a few months she started to lean on you about getting a job. That started a whole chain of events that wound up with you going to work every day at some terrible low-wage job. The money you did make went to paying the rent for an apartment that you didn't need when you were single and living in your friend's basement, but that was essential in the eyes of your new girlfriend. And if all that wasn't bad enough, your new girlfriend took up so much of your time that you were lucky to spend even one night a week smoking crack with whores up on Aurora Avenue. But they loved Mike nonetheless, and he had come back around when that new girl had gotten sick of him. What could you do? It happened to everybody at some point, and for most people at numerous points over the course of their lives.

Ron had been around, though. He might as well have lived at Jack's place, too. He had been on the couch about half the week. Officially, he had been living with his dad about eight blocks away. Apparently, he'd even had a job as a DJ in a strip club. At least, that's what he had told his dad. In fact, he had just dealt drugs to strippers at the sleazy strip joints on South Tacoma Way. Drugs that Jack had fronted him. Drugs that Jack had fronted him in great abundance due to his chronic lack of funds to make large purchases on his own. Despite being chronically broke, Jack had established a level of trust with Ron. Ron had been part of the inner circle. He might have ripped you off, but he'd never have ripped off Jack, Todd, or Mike. He had always made good when he moved his product. Even on the rare occasions when he had overindulged on his fronted product, and hadn't been able to make good right then, he had owed Jack and made good the next time around. He'd certainly had to step on his supply more than normal to make those ends meet, but he always paid Jack off eventually.

Things had been out of control over there. Jack had pretty well owned PLU and the town's drug trade, but cops had still been a problem. As far as Jack knew, they hadn't known who he was or what he was up to. They hadn't for a while, but eventually they had. Cops were stupid, but even a blind squirrel found the nut eventually. Making money had been the easy part. As long as Jack had had access to suppliers with large quantities, the customers had beat a path to his door. And with the quantities he had moved on a regular basis, he had established an unblemished reputation with most of the manufacturers and suppliers in Pierce County— the ones that counted anyway.

In 1989, the crank had come from the bikers out in the southeast of the county. The bikers had known all the burned-out sixties flower children who kept Jack in psychedelics, and the hippies had known the Mexicans over in Salishan's shack city that dealt the best blow and weed. While those channels were solid, the crack had been the most reliable hookup. It had come from the gangbangers in Tacoma's hilltop neighborhood, good quality too. The bikers had made their own crank, so the quality was always inconsistent, but the supply was always abundant. The hippies had made their own LSD and picked the mushrooms they sold. They'd had some weed too, but not as much as the Mexicans. Who knows where the Mexicans had gotten the blow and weed, but most of the time buying from them was cool. It had been a hodgepodge of suppliers, and it hadn't always been consistent, but most of the time it had worked out.

The crack, on the other hand, had been too easy to acquire. Thanks to the Los Angeles to Tacoma I-5 pipeline, there had always been crack to purchase. Jack had had one hookup with the Mexicans, and two or three with the bikers and hippies, but he had been able to go to a dozen gangbangers he knew on Hilltop for crack in quantity. It was like those heavenly white rocks had just tumbled down off Hilltop into Jack's backyard. He had felt like a lucky prospector who had hit a vein that never stopped producing.

One day, knocking at the door had roused Jack from a mid-afternoon slumber. That was weird. Usually, his afternoon naps had been disturbed by the phone ringing, the other end of the line sure to be an agitated, strung-out college kid. It was always that, or Todd knocking things over in the front room. Strange visitors had always been calling cards of change, and Jack was about to go through the biggest life change to date.

"Stop knockin' already, my fuckin' head hurts. Unless of course you're the cops, in which case, just kick the fuckin' door in already."

"Open the door, Jack," the familiar female voice had said on the other side.

In a moment he'd placed the voice. It was Beth, the LPN that he'd only just begun to fall in love with during his first stay at Western State. It had taken a moment longer than it should have for him to remember to look through the peephole and verify what his mind had just registered. The feeling that it was the S.W.A.T. team outside had still been a little unshakeable. In Jack's mind, the idea that she might have been working with the cops had also been a possibility, but one that he had been willing to overlook, or at least chalk up to meth paranoia. Whatever paranoid suspicions he had harbored, he had still wanted to see her, and he had flung open the door without another thought of arrest.

"Wow, you're a sight for sore beer goggles." Jack had thought that line was clever, but Beth hadn't.

"Try taking the goggles off once in a while and

looking through clear eyes, Jack. This place is gross," she'd said.

"You're just jealous that I'm living the dream and you're stuck working at that nuthouse. Don't you know? I'm the king of Parkland. Now that my queen has arrived, my kingdom is complete."

"Great kingdom!" Her sarcasm had not been hidden. "You do grandiosity well, and if your throne wasn't covered in empty 40oz bottles and hamburger wrappers I might consider sitting on it."

"Sorry 'bout that. Let me clean that off for you, madame. The staff are kind of bastards 'bout picking up around the kingdom. The king winds up doing most of the janitorial detail, which as you can see is very little"

"The house isn't the only thing that could use some cleaning up." She had attached no sarcasm to that comment.

"What, I stink or something?"

"Yeah, you kind of do. You're looking sort of rough, boy. The only reason I was able to find you is because you gave this as your new address before you stopped coming to your outpatient group. I hope you appreciate the effort I made to dig you up. They'd fire me if anybody found out I was poking around in your files."

"But you never worried 'bout poking around with me while I was a patient?"

"That was different."

"Why!"

"Because I always had a plan if we got caught."

"Really?"

"Yep, I'd just tell the staff that you were raping me. Then they'd have kept you at the hospital, where I could look after you forever instead of worrying about you being out here on your own."

"But your plan is flawed. What if you lost your job?"

"What flaws? There aren't any, not when a girl is in love. If I lost my job, I could just get committed to the hospital. Either way, we'd be together," she'd said in a sweet tone of voice that had let Jack know that she was sincere.

All this while they'd been inching closer to the front room and toward the couch. The hospitable thing to do would have been to ask her if she'd like a beverage, which Jack had done in a halfhearted tone of voice. She had been there to have a talk, to straighten Jack out, and to put him back on course. Maybe even to rescue him, if she needed to, but that wasn't all that she had been there for. She'd worn that outfit before. Jack had almost never seen her in anything but scrubs. At the hospital, most of the staff had worn jeans and t-shirts, but Beth hadn't liked blending in with the patients, so she had always worn scrubs. Once in a while, she had come in to get something she had forgotten, or just to say hi to everybody on a day off.

The day Jack had seen her wearing that plaid miniskirt with the black button-up sweater and knee-high white stockings, she had been going to a Cramps show. Her makeup had been all-white foundation and black eye makeup, like a China doll. The normally chocolate brown bobbed hair had been turned jet black, and she'd ratted it until it stood out in the shape of a mushroom cap. To top off the ensemble, she had worn John Fluevog creepers with points that stuck out three sizes farther than her actual feet. When she had come in on her day off all dolled up, her excuse had been that she left her makeup bag there. Of course, her face had told the story of a woman who was already makeup bag equipped. Also, Beth had never worn makeup at work, further calling her story into question, but all girls liked to show off a little bit sometimes.

Jack hadn't been able to think about anything but that outfit for a week. Then, there she'd been, identical to that day. The only exceptions had been that the hair and makeup were both toned down a little bit.

She had been trying to make a point, to make Jack see the error of his ways, but her concentration had dropped through the floor. She had been fidgeting and wouldn't look him in the eye. She had licked her lips, and in less than two minutes she'd managed to lick most of her lipstick off. In her mind, she had wrestled with her conscience. She had wanted to do something, but needed to say something. Jack had decided to let her off the hook. After all, he had figured, she'd have plenty of time to talk later. She had finally locked eyes with him when she had felt his hand sliding up her skirt. She had started kissing him, and they had descended onto the couch. Jack's first thought had been, *where is Todd?* Todd was always sitting right where they were making out. Wherever Todd had been that day, he had picked a great time to be absent.

The first time, they hadn't made it off the couch; they hadn't even made it all the way out of their clothes. Beth's thong had been dangling around one of her stocking-covered ankles. Her bra had been unclasped so her breasts could peek out the bottom of it, and other than that she had been fully clothed. Jack's pants and boxers had been around his ankles, and with a shirt and effectively no pants, he had looked like Winnie the Pooh fucking the honey jar. Afterward, Beth had buckled her bra, and then it had been talking time again. Jack still hadn't been ready to have that talk. He had been able to distract her with some post-coital grinding, and then they had been going at it again. That time they had actually ended up in Jack's bed. They had also managed to get all of their clothes off, except for Beth's stockings. The stockings were hot, and Jack had made a point of leaving them right where they were.

Jack had done his best to postpone the conversation she'd come there to have, but after fucking twice, he had been out of energy, out of semen, and out of excuses to not have the conversation.

"So, do you have any little college girlfriends out here?" She had said it like she couldn't care less, but he had known it was a serious question.

"You know how I feel 'bout you," he'd said.

"I thought I did, but then you pulled your disappearing act."

"Me, I don't even know your address!"

"But you knew my phone number, and you were supposed to be at the hospital every week for outpatient group."

"And I went."

"Yeah, for two whole weeks. And if you want to drop out of your outpatient program that's your business, but I said to call when you got settled. You have to understand that being involved with you outside of work is at the very best frowned upon, at worst, I'd get fucking fired. I didn't want to interfere, so I waited. And then I waited some more, even after you stopped group. You made me cry, Jack, and now I figure you're going to do it again."

"And again, and again, and again," he'd said.

"What are you going to do out here, Jack? I mean, I can guess what you're doing, but how long do you think this is going to hold out? How long do you think you can maintain this before you end up right back at Western State, or in prison?"

Jack had said, "What do you want me to tell you?"

"I don't know, but you need to tell me something. You're not the one who drove out here not knowing what sort of reaction you'd get. For all I know, I was just your little nurse fling while you were committed. Just the only girl you could fuck while you were locked up, and then you disappear after you're out. What would you think?"

"I'd think I was a dickhead. That's exactly what I've been. I love you. I think you're the only person I've ever loved for the right reasons. I just forgot 'bout you. That sounds mean, but that's not how I mean it. Everything out here is just so loud, and you're quiet. You got lost in the noise, but I want you more than any of this stuff."

"You have to get out of here. You're not on your meds, there is non-discreet paraphernalia from at least three illegal drugs in plain sight. I don't know what else is going on over here, but if you want me you've got to clean up."

"What can I do? This is my house. I can't just leave. How am I supposed to make money? It's not like I can just walk out, get a newspaper, and find a job making twenty thousand a year."

"Just come, just pack up and leave this place with me. Do what you've got to do, square away what you've got to square away, and get the fuck out of here. We can figure out the details later, but I know you've got to do this now."

Looking at Jack's life from the outside, it probably hadn't seemed like much to leave behind. There hadn't been anything of value that he owned in that house, nothing but his drug stash. He hadn't even owned the house; he had barely owned the Volvo. But it had still been his house, and his life, and his friends, and his lucrative drug dealing business. Despite the illegal nature of his enterprise, he had still felt more in control of his own destiny than at any other time in his life. But, besides that, there had been his friends, the real ones. Good or bad, they had never left Jack in the lurch. How could he have left them behind then? Going with Beth would have meant leaving them, and even though nobody had said it out loud, it had been more obvious than the bullet holes Todd put in his door jamb.

"One week, that's how long it will take me to square things away here. I think Todd and Ron can take over the lease on this place, and there are some loose ends with people I've got to take care of before I can leave."

Beth had said, "I don't think I want to know

anything about what you have to do, do I?"

"I doubt it."

"Just don't do anything stupid, don't get caught. Just do what you have to, and if you make me cry this time, I won't come looking for you again."

Chapter 3

J ack had always wondered if anyone else suffered from chronic nose dehydration. He had figured people had it when it was cold and dry, but not all the time like him. It wasn't some paranoid delusion, either. "My nostrils are never fuckin' clear. There's always snot and boogers, but my nostrils are all dry. These boogers are always hard as rocks, and they're stuck to the walls of my Mojave Desert nostrils like barnacles on a ship's hull."

Jack had been given one week to shed his skin, to become another human being entirely. There had been work to be done, but he had been determined to see it through. As they had been throughout his entire life, the core members of his adopted family, his crew, had been supportive of what he was trying to do. Mike had followed a somewhat similar path with a more domesticated existence away from the action that centered around Jack's place. Todd and Ron, always optimistic, had realized that Jack wouldn't be going away forever. It was just a hiatus from the action. A vacation, or a leave of absence, a sabbatical if you will, and that just like any other cohesive unit they'd always be pulled back together again when circumstances warranted. That was how it always worked. Their bonds were those of family, and families rallied around each other in times of need. Even when the bonds had been strained, they didn't break.

As Jack had expected, Todd and Ron had taken over the rental agreement on the abandoned house. Jack had decided to leave all his furniture, dishes, and TV behind to square things financially with them for his bailing in the middle of the month. Not that things had to be squared with them, since there was plenty of money around that house to go around, but Jack hadn't needed the stuff, and it was what they would have done for him if the situation had been reversed.

"It wasn't like I was goin' to the moon. Parkland was just a suburb of Tacoma, and Beth's apartment was right in the Stadium District of Tacoma, near downtown. It wasn't no more than fifteen minutes' drive from Parkland." Geographically, it had been pretty close, but it was certainly a change of scenery.

Even in a small city like Tacoma, it was very easy to start your life over again. It was amazing, but right on the other side of town, under the assumed shroud of a normal person, you could live somewhat anonymously. Drug kingpin of Parkland, psychotic weirdo in south Tacoma, but up the road in the Stadium District, just some guy living with his girlfriend.

Elements of his previous lives had been around as he prepared his exit, and he had still run into people, but he mostly chose to ignore them, and they tended to ignore him back. People had picked up on that vibe, and mostly respected it. Most of the time, no words had been exchanged at all, and when they had been, they rarely went beyond a simple "hello" or "what you been up to." The only people that had never gotten the brush-off from Jack were the closest of the close. Dealers, fienders, mooches, one-night stands, acquaintances, they could all get fucked, Jack had no loyalty to them. Only Todd, Mike, and Ron had been exempt from this brush-off.

There hadn't turned out to be as much to take care of as he'd originally thought, and he had spent most of the week getting high with Todd and Ron. Some local college upstarts had wanted to get some business of their own going. They'd had plenty of cash, so Jack had agreed to broker a couple of big money deals for them that had netted about forty-five hundred for himself. He'd known that, on top of what he'd saved up, this windfall would keep him luxuriously unemployed for at least six or seven more months.

He had also put together some deals to set up Ron and Todd, from which he had taken no finder's fee. He hadn't wanted to make a profit off of them. He'd wanted them to be comfortable. Before he'd set the college kids up, he had made sure it wouldn't hurt Ron and Todd's business endeavors. If it had, the college boys would have been out of luck. Jack wouldn't have sold out his crew.

Ron had made his money off the strippers at the strip clubs on South Tacoma Way. Todd had been much less ambitious, choosing to stick with a smaller, exclusive clientele that hadn't really consisted of the college students. You had to admire the lack of greediness Todd had exhibited, even if it had been motivated by laziness. His theory of life had been that of the comfortable minimalist, who, even with the tools at his disposal to make a great fortune, was content to work only enough to get by. He had been Buddha with a glass pipe. To Todd, everything had been fine as long as there was food in the fridge, the rent was paid, there was the occasional piece of ass, and, most importantly, the drugs were in the stash box. Todd could exhibit restraint on a level Jack would call otherworldly, except when it came to using drugs. In that respect, his restraint had been nonexistent.

They'd had a party the night before Jack moved

out. Jack had already moved everything he had intended to over to Beth's earlier that day. All he had brought was his safe, his records, and his clothes. She had still been on swing shift at the hospital, so she had stopped by the house before work that afternoon. All the people that Jack would henceforth ignore when he saw them had filled the abandoned house by two in the afternoon. Everyone had known that when there was a party at the abandoned house, there'd be plenty of free drugs to go around. Jack couldn't have cared less why they had showed up. He had known he'd be gone before midnight. The original plan had been to head over to Beth's the next afternoon after he'd slept off that night's events, but after she'd stopped by, he had known he wanted to get to her apartment so that they could sleep in the same bed that very night. She hadn't said so, but Jack had been able to tell that she was uneasy about the party.

On the other hand, Jack had been anything but uneasy. All those leeches that had infested the abandoned house at that moment had filled him with anticipation for his new life. He had looked into their hollow eyes, and their rudderless existences, and been grateful to be leaving a similar existence behind. If he hadn't known it before, he had known it that afternoon. He had known he had nothing in common with those people. He had known that everything up until then had just been a terribly low interval in what was going to be a long life. He had known they only liked him because he was the dope man. He'd always done the same thing with everyone except Ron, Todd, Mike, and, now, Beth. When the crank and coke left, so would they.

They were shells of people that had functioned mostly as life support systems for their drug addictions. Other people hadn't mattered to them, not even their own families, and they had been incapable of having real relationships with other people. He had literally prayed that day that he would have the strength to stop being one of them.

Every time someone had asked Jack where he was going away to, he had made up a new story. Jack had told Jill he was going to Tibet to become a monk. He had told Larry that he was getting locked up for a couple of years for selling stolen AK-47's. Bobby had thought Jack was going to Amsterdam with his earnings to become a pimp and hash mogul.

To each plastic person, Jack had spun a different tale, and, oddly enough, not one person at the party had noticed that Jack had told at least twenty different stories about where he was going. He had known they didn't give a shit about him, but all those fienders were so self-absorbed they hadn't even bothered to talk to one another. "Jesus, what do those fuckers even talk about when they're getting' high together?" Not one of those people had actually cared where Jack was going. Without speaking out loud, every one of them had indicated that they really didn't want to know where he was going, and that the only reason they had asked in the first place was because it had been his going away party. On the other hand, if the free crack and booze moved away, Jack suspected everyone would have been genuinely curious about where they moved to.

The only reason Jack had even been there was that his real friends had wanted to give him a party, and he had been there to spend a few last hours with them before setting out on his own. Jack hadn't really even liked parties that much. He'd always viewed a party as a means of getting drunk, high, or laid—all three, preferably. At any given party, if he could convince a girl to leave with him as soon as he arrived while also grabbing a bottle of Jack and scoring some blow, he had been content to ditch the whole affair altogether. Even when he had stayed at parties, he had typically just held court with two or three close confidants. Most importantly, Jack could get drunk, high, and laid without the help of a party at all. Parties were places that mostly just enabled those less skilled at procuring vice in the normal world to get fucked, baked, and smashed. Again, Jack hadn't needed the party; Jack was skilled at hunting for his vice in the wild. He hadn't shot fish in barrels.

That night, even Mike had come out, which had pleased Jack for a variety of reasons. It had reaffirmed that they were still a crew, and always would be. Mike had been scarce since moving in with his girlfriend, and Jack would soon be doing the same thing. Mike had been Jack's closest friend, and at that point, of the four of them, he had become the most distanced from Jack. Jack had known it would most likely stay that way, with the both of them now domesticated. Seeing Todd and Ron wouldn't be too hard when he needed to. They would be there, slinging, sleeping, or partying, and Jack could always make an excuse to come out there once or twice a month for a couple of hours. He had known it wouldn't be the same, but it was something. With Mike, though, it had been different. Todd and Ron hadn't even met Mike's girlfriend, and Jack had only been to their house once. Jack had known it could be the last time he saw Mike for a year. They had rehashed their entire life, adolescent criminal careers to present circumstances, in about three hours.

Mike was the best and worst fighter Jack had ever known. He had excelled at starting fights, and sucked at finishing them. He had also been Jack's best friend, and the best friend to have around when you needed something. His loyalty had often run into conflict with his erratic impulses, which could sometimes simultaneously make him the worst best friend in the world. Mike was a man who was most easily recognizable by his small stature and strange behaviors, but, more than those, he was recognizable by his passion for protecting those closest to him.

When Jack was twelve-years-old, his mom had put him into Keithley Junior High in Parkland because she hadn't wanted him going to his assigned school, the bad school, Baker Junior High, in south Tacoma. It was an ironic choice, since Parkland had in actuality been more blighted than his own neighborhood. The first person he had met at his new school was Mike. Since they had only been twelve, Mike's small stature hadn't been evident yet, but the behavior had been just as strange, and the even stranger look on his face had made Jack wonder about him. He had always seemed like a guy on the brink of doing something stupid. Within a couple of days of their meeting, Mike had proved that it hadn't just been a look, and that he really *was* always on the brink of doing something stupid.

Jack had met Mike when he was on a two-or-three-day lull from erratic outbursts, but it hadn't taken long before his true colors had begun to shine through. The first noteworthy thing they had ever done together was get the shit kicked out of them.

At the time, Jack hadn't even really known Mike at all. He had just been the first guy that Mike talked to at his new school. Those people, the first guys, were like transitional or rebound friends. They never lasted and were really just there so that you had someone to talk to until you made some real friends.

This guy who Jack hadn't really known, and hadn't been convinced that he really wanted to know, had started their friendship by agitating and ultimately punching some kid whose size would have made him a big adult despite the fact that he was in seventh grade. He hadn't been an adult, but instead a gigantic twelve-year-old. Early onset puberty, Jack guessed. The first thing Jack had done as Mike's friend was get his ass handed to him for trying to pull someone off Mike. Jack couldn't say that he'd seen Mike win more fights than he'd lost, but he could say that when Mike had been around, Jack had never had to get his ass kicked alone. Mike had picked fights with opponents like he preferred getting beat down to winning. If true, it would explain why he had picked such big guys to brawl with. Sometimes, he had picked big women to brawl with, but those tended to be prostitutes he had refused to pay.

One way or the other, the beating that the testosterone-infused seventh grader dealt them had bonded them for life, and their crew had been born right then and there. Jack had already been friends with Todd, as Todd's family had been Mormon, too. Ron had actually lived up the street from Mike, so they had already known each other as well. Before long, Ron and Todd had folded into what Mike and Jack had begun that day, and Jack and Mike had become the genesis of what would eventually be an unbreakable crew.

Mike had been the beginning of real disobedience for Jack, and Mike had kept Jack in trouble on a pretty much daily basis until, after many suspensions and trips to the juvenile detention facility, they had both been expelled from Washington High School. Jack had been a misbehaved child before that, but together Mike and Jack had taken it into the realm of incorrigible. It had been the end of both of their scholastic careers, and with Ron and Todd dropping out shortly thereafter, it had been the beginning of an age of realization for all of them. Their families had been forced to put up with them to varying degrees. That they had all been great disappointments to their families was clear. But the four of them had chosen each other to self-destruct with. It had been around that time they had all realized that they had more than just passing friendships.

Jack was a blackout drinker and had been from the start. From that first bottle of Mad Dog 20/20 when he was a kid, booze had always kicked his ass, and he couldn't remember a minute of it. Nothing had been like that night with his first bottle of Orange Jubilee all those years ago. The bottle in Jack's hand always brought the blackout—but nothing brought the newness back—nothing. That had been what always happened, and just to reiterate, it had happened *every* time Jack drank. Sometimes, if he snorted enough crank, it had taken longer to blackout, but it had always happened eventually.

Why Jack had been sitting outside a mobile home he was familiar with, situated in a small rural town known as Kapowsin, on a wooded piece of property, was beyond him. Coming out of blackouts in strange places was just a part of life if you were a blackout drinker. Missing time and lack of judgment also came along with the territory. The last thing Jack remembered was having shot the shit with Mike at the abandoned house. That had been about six-thirty in the evening. It had been three-thirty, then, according to his watch and the clock on the dash of the Volvo. Considering that it was pitch-black outside, Jack had assumed three-thirty meant three-thirty in the morning.

On rare occasions, Jack had lost entire days in blackouts, but usually it had been like that night. He'd regularly lose eight, maybe twelve, hours. Sometimes Jack had been able to tell he'd been awake the whole time and had snapped out of it, but more often he'd woken up after being passed out somewhere, at which point he'd made his way to his bed or car, whichever was closer. Sometimes it had taken a while for him to find his keys. Sometimes, if he was near his car, he'd driven home right away and slept it off for most of the next day. A lot of times, he hadn't been able to get the key in the ignition, so he'd just slept it off for a few hours in his car. Sometimes, he had been outside the car and unable to get the keys in the door lock, and he'd had to sleep it off next to his car. Sometimes, he hadn't been able to get the key into his door lock at home, and he'd slept it off next to his door. Among other things, this was one of the recurring themes in Jack's life that he had hoped to be saying goodbye to.

Every blackout was different. You wouldn't think so, since alcoholics had little to no recollection of what happened during them. The lack of memory was the same, but the bruises on your body were different. The grass stains on your clothes were different. The dents on your car were different. The looks you got from friends and coworkers were different. Where you woke up was very different. Most of all, that gut feeling when you woke up was always different. Your gut gave you a feel for how things had gone during the blackout. Sometimes, the gut feeling was pretty good, like when you woke up next to an attractive girl in her underwear. Sometimes, the gut feeling was pretty bad, like when you woke up next to an unattractive girl in her underwear.

Good or bad—and for Jack it had usually been bad—you wanted to solve the mystery of the night before. Human beings can't leave a mystery alone. Mysteries beg to be solved; otherwise, why would they leave so many clues around for you to find? Things either felt right, or they didn't. When they didn't was when you started calling your friends and asking what happened the night before. It was those days when you rolled over at two in the afternoon and looked under the bed to make sure there wasn't a dead hooker down there. Jack had used to find cards from the police with incident numbers on them shoved in the cellophane wrapper of his cigarette packs. Had he been the assailant or victim? He had rarely found out, since he had never called the precinct to inquire about the circumstances of the various incidents.

The first thing Jack had always attempted to determine was if he was in his own bed or automobile. If not, he had next determined if he was somewhere he recognized. Often times, he had just been passed out on a friend's couch. After he turned twenty-one it had become routine to find Jack crashed out in a booth at one of his regular bars.

He'd had a lot of bad feelings waking up from blackouts, but he'd never actually woken up next to a dead hooker. He did have blackouts where he seriously thought he might. Sitting outside of that mobile home that night had given Jack the eeriest feeling he'd ever had. Ever. Normally, when he came to and felt anything remotely disturbing, he'd get the fuck out of there that very second and figure it all out later. Jack loved solving the mystery as much as anyone, but he valued staying alive and out of jail even more. For whatever reason, on that night, he had needed to sit there in that driveway and take in the scene. There had been lights on in the mobile home, a truck in the driveway, and motorcycles under the carport. The bikers that lived there had dealt crank. He was quite familiar with that place.

There had been no light to see by, just the one on in the mobile home. "We call 'em trailers." Waking up hadn't necessarily sobered Jack up. He had still been quite drunk, and lighting a smoke had seemed like the thing to do. There was no way he would have gone up to the trailer door and asked what happened, not the way he had felt. For all he knew, someone inside would have just stuck a shotgun in his face. Maybe he had slept with one of the nasty crank whores who regularly congregated around that mobile home. He hadn't known. They had come for the free tweak, and the bikers had let them stay because they put out.

Maybe they had kicked the shit out of him and then shoved him in his car. He was terrified and hadn't wanted to go up to the house, but he had also felt strongly compelled to stay put for the time being. After a few minutes, Jack had started building a likely narrative in his head. He had probably pissed someone inside off. It just happened like that. Jack drank, and people around him got pissed at him. He hadn't been in pain, which meant nobody had actually kicked the shit out of him, and they'd let him pass out in his car. Or they'd put him in his car when he passed out. Either way, they'd let him be out there for who knew how many hours, so he had felt safe as long as he stayed quiet. He had killed his smoke and dusted off the last swig of the 40oz that he'd woken up with between his legs before taking a leak in the driveway. "Warm malt liquor might as well be piss, but still if that's all there is to drink." There hadn't been any more beer in the car, and Jack had almost been out of smokes, but he had been able to get the key in the ignition. It was definitely time to go.

If it hadn't been for the drastic changes about to happen in his life, he may have dwelled on what might have happened with those bikers in the trailer. After all, they'd been one of his main connections for meth, but, driving to Beth's, he had tried to tell himself that he didn't give a shit. Really, he had given a shit. He had known that something bad had happened in there, and that it could have been anything from a dead hooker to unprotected sex with the HIV-positive girl Cheryl that hung around that place.

He wasn't going to be buying from them anymore, and he had tried to put that trailer in the rearview literally and figuratively that night. If he could have shaken that sick feeling in the pit of his stomach, he'd never have given those fuckhead bikers another thought, but he hadn't been able to.

Jack never stopped thinking about what happened in that trailer that night, not for the rest of his life. It was one of those things that had taken a piece of his soul permanently. He had never lived another carefree day after that. The idea that whatever had happened in that trailer that night would creep up on him from behind someday had loomed large as he drove.

Chapter 4

"This seems like a good place to start a new chapter. Pause for dramatic effect. One of the most annoyin' things 'bout listenin' to a story is when the storyteller butchers an otherwise interestin' tale by not knowin' when to take a breath and pivot. My friend Robert—who was a great drinkin' buddy—always did that. Robert wasn't never part of the crew, but he was a reliable alcoholic who you could always count on for smokes, jokes, and beers. Plus, he really did have a crazy story for just about any occasion. It was just his delivery that killed them stories of his.

"Knowin' when to pause is a gift, and since that trailer was the end of one chapter, it makes sense that the drive away from it was the beginnin' of the next. It didn't take no brains to start this chapter exactly where it belonged. Even Robert could have managed this transition without butcherin' it."

The drive to Beth's had only half existed to Jack. He had been foggy, but no longer blacked out.

Still, the inability to track events during that drive had persisted. Most of the time, his green Volvo rambled along the streets like a little tank. Jack's blackouts had always ensured that a certain amount of property damage was done while he was driving. Mailboxes beware. Garbage cans and parked cars hadn't fared much better. Curbs, unfortunately, didn't move when you hit them, and the Volvo's rims and steering alignment told the tale of many such impacts. But this hadn't been a blackout. He was fairly sober by then, certainly no longer in a blackout. He had felt more like something had highjacked his mind, leaving him only enough brainpower to successfully pilot the Volvo. He simply hadn't been able to put one single thought together. Nothing had stuck, no matter how hard he concentrated.

Beth had lived in the Stadium District north of downtown Tacoma. The building was an oddity. In a very old part of town where most of the apartment buildings were built in the twenties, Beth's building had looked like something Mike Brady had designed in the seventies, complete with a hideous sandstone masonry facade. It had those flat, non-uniform bricks that sandwiched in three floors of apartments with railed-in outdoor walkways. Jack had been puzzled by this, and the thousands of other apartment buildings like this. Somewhere, somebody in the seventies had thought apartment buildings should look like cheap motels in the desert. The really surprising thing to Jack was that the idea had caught on.

The seventies was a lost decade, overshadowed by the sixties, and quaint in the shadow of the big eighties. Like a middle child stuck in-between the relative flamboyance and success of its more successful siblings, it tried to stand out by dressing itself up in ridiculous getups. Beth's building was a prime example of goofy seventies getups. Those cars, that architecture—what the fuck were those people thinking? Even the seventies would look at some of the stuff it had worn and say, "What the fuck was I thinking?" The cars had finally started to disappear, but places like Beth's apartment hadn't yet become shabby enough for people to start knocking them down, so they were still living with the legacy of that architecture for the moment. And living with Beth meant Jack would be living with it wall to wall.

The other structures in Beth's neighborhood had been huge Victorian houses, mostly converted to multi-family units, or the aforementioned apart-ment buildings from the twenties. They had been in a state between disrepair and renovation. It was a time well before those sorts of neighborhoods and homes had become sought after by the droves of tech migrants that would flood Puget Sound in the decades to come. They hadn't even yet been appreciated for their sturdiness, or workmanship. The huge maples canopying the cobblestone streets in these neighborhoods north of downtown had always made Jack feel like he was in a Norman Rockwell painting. It was in the city, but not in the shit. Just like those paintings, the mischievousness had been there, but it had been cloaked by the serenity that patriotic normality brought

Driving across Washington State was an interesting experience. If you were headed to Puget Sound, which let's face it, if you're coming to Washington, you're definitely coming to Puget Sound, and you entered the state in the southeast you would find yourself in a desert.

You were also in the breadbasket of the state. More precisely, you were in the applecart of the state. Everything grew in southeast Washington. Apples grew there, sure, but do you like beer? If so, there's a pretty good chance the hops used to brew that beer came from there.How about grapes, yeah seriously grapes—and more than a few wine operations. Cherries, grapes, strawberries, blueberries—all there. In fact, Washington's fruit game was beyond reproach.

But you couldn't stop there; you had to see the Columbia River, too. If you were west of the

Rockies, it was very possible that your power came from there. Eventually, you had to cross the Cascade Mountains. People in the east didn't know what a mountain was supposed to look like. The ones in Washington were covered in snow and trees. Their angled rocks looked like they could cut diamond.

After that, you were almost to Puget Sound, which had a nautical culture in the purest sense of the word. If you made it that far, you'd have come a long way across the state, and you still wouldn't have seen the peninsula, the San Juans, the coast, or the Olympic Mountains, to name only a few.

In the future, transplants would flock in droves to this nirvana. They would dress up in garments that said Columbia Sportswear, Patagonia, Land's End, REI, and The North Face. They would have kayaks and snowboards mounted to the racks atop their Subarus. Sometimes, they would have the kayaks and snowboards on top of the Subarus at the same time, tempting locals like Jack to wonder what the hell was going on. "Cause that guy can't use the kayak on the mountain, and he can't use the snowboard on the sound. Where's that fuckin' guy goin' today? Why is he wearin' a windbreaker and a beanie? It's July!"

That was the future, but the present had been Maple pitch all over the cars parked by Jack's Volvo. Under those Maples was the best view of

Commencement Bay in the city. Jack had liked to sit in the Volvo and look at the bay. Jack hadn't intuited it at the time, but at some point, in the future, he'd be sitting in that very spot on the road and there'd be a condo building obstructing his view of the bay. Based on how things had been going in the late eighties, he could have told you then that the future condo building would probably have a kayak and snowboard strapped to the top of it.

What only occurred to him many years later as he again sat in that spot, this time with the condominium towering over him, was that his home town didn't wait on his permission to do anything just because he had been born there. The city changed, and, yes, people from other places moved in, built things, got married, drove Subarus, and made lives for themselves right there. Jack had no ownership or veto power over who could live there, or what they might build or drive when they came. That condo would be built to house the new northwest.

Soon, the professional class of the new technology revolution would be there in force. That future condo building would tower like some new stylish company town housing the laborers of the new economy. Jack would just be a victim of progress, that was all—him and a million other unhappy sots that had come before him. The northwest would leave him behind.

Seventy years ago, some guy on the next block up the hill had probably sat on the porch of his Victorian home as the first bricks had been laid for the new, but now retro, apartment building next to Beth's. He had probably said to himself, "An apartment building, now, that's definitely going to wreck my view of Commencement Bay." And that guy had been right; his view of the bay had been wrecked, and the city had gone on in spite of his feelings about it. Jack had just never realized it until that condo showed up in the mid-nineties. That was Jack's future. Enjoying the bay for a few more minutes from the lumpy driver's seat of the Volvo before he went into Beth's place had been Jack's present. It seemed cliché, but he had watched the sun rise anyway.

When Jack had crawled into bed next to Beth, he had imagined that the sunrise was the cleansing dawn of his new life, or some spiritual-sounding bullshit like that. Jack could be sentimental about things like new dawns, clean sheets, and dropped charges. For the first time in a long time, maybe the first time ever, he had daydreamed about what life could be like with another person. Drool had run out of the corner of his mouth and onto to Beth's soft, clean pillowcase, and he had felt himself starting to snore as he dropped off into a chemical-induced coma.

While he slept, he had dreamed about this show at the OK Hotel a few nights prior. It was a dream that seemed realistic both during sleep and after he had woken up. It hadn't been bizarre. It hadn't had weird imagery that only made sense while the dream was happening but then turned into incomprehensible nonsense the moment you woke up. It had been a dream about the other night. Everything had happened just the way it had really happened that night. That had been the weird part—no dream-state weirdness. It had basically just been reliving the night.

Portland was Seattle's violent little brother. Olympia was its bratty little sister. Vancouver B.C. was the cousin that you always wanted to come to parties because he brought beer and field hockey equipment. Tacoma was the uncle that you grudgingly let in because he had good drugs. The other night at the OK Hotel had been Portland's night, and he had come looking for a fight.

It had been three days before, and it had been the one date Beth and Jack had gone on during his week of preparation for moving in with her. Just getting to the OK Hotel had been an adventure. It was under the Alaskan Way Viaduct, right next to the piers. The space under the viaduct wasn't good for anything except parking, and it was the shabbiest parking area in the city. Violent crack-addicted homeless people had haunted that place. You were bound to get jumped and robbed eventually if you were around there long enough, but if you weren't paying attention, it was likely to happen sooner rather than later.

Outside the gig there had been some goofy-looking kid spare changing, even though he was wearing brand new Doc Martens and a two-hundred-dollar leather jacket. The Poison Idea t-shirt he had worn looked like he'd just bought it at Fallout Records and put it on before the show. He had probably only been a year or two younger than Jack, but those years that each had lived could not have been more different. Jack had grown up thirsty and miserable; this guy had been some rich kid on LSD. Jack had given him a dollar because he felt sorry for him. Jack had felt like the kid was definitely going to get killed inside the show, and begging for money, money he didn't need, outside the show, would not endear him to anyone inside.

Jack had spent most of the show trying to sit at the coffee bar in the front of the place. Trying being the key word. If he had moved one cheek off his stool, there'd have been someone else's cheek trying to squeeze in, but it had still been roomier than standing next to the stage. When he had finally been forced to give up his stool, he had gone outside and drank the beers he'd stashed under the viaduct before the show. Jack had seen Nausea several times—Date Rape, too—but he'd only seen Poison Idea once. Jack had been trying to build up his liquid courage for the PI set.

Back inside, people had gotten bloody, and the guitarist, Pig Champion, had sat on a little wooden chair that looked like the sort you found in kindergarten classrooms. Maybe it was a normal size chair, but his mass had dwarfed it. Jack really didn't know. Pig Champion wasn't just a name; the man had to have been six-hundred pounds. Jack's brain had been just the right amount of distorted for this. He had been full of beers, but not blacked out. Squeezing into the mass of sweaty flesh had ensured that he didn't get bloated or have to piss. It had been a like a sauna, sapping any excess moisture from him.

The band had played a song called "Say Goodbye" for the sweaty masses. The air in that damp dark space had been so humid that Jack could have sworn he wasn't breathing air at all, but instead moisture, literally inhaling the beverages, cigarettes, and life forces of those around him encapsulated in airborne water vapor.

It had all been background noise to him, though. Swimming their way through the beer his brain was floating in all his fears of how his life would be with

Beth. Every time he had looked across the hall at Beth, he had been amazed how she stood out in that crowd, as if she was three dimensions of full, vibrant color, and everything else was two dimensions in black and white. Then it had happened.

Punk rock shows and the northwest in general had suffered from a terrible affliction. That had been neo-Nazi skinheads. The bands hadn't been racist, the punks hadn't been racist—shit even most of the skinheads hadn't been racist—but those wannabe Nazi fuckers had still come to the shows. They had come to cause trouble at shows, record stores, parks, coffee shops, and bars.

This particular skinhead, Adam, had been well-known in their local scene for the troublemaker he was. On his way to the front of the stage, he had slammed into Beth so hard she had disappeared from Jack's view momentarily. It turned out he'd slammed into her so hard she had been knocked onto her hands and knees. This happened con-stantly at punk shows. In front, where people were slam dancing, it was expected. It wasn't the fact that it had happened. It wasn't even the fact that he had failed to help her up. It was the fact that the neo-Nazi piece of shit had laughed as he did it. His presence at every show was always an omnipresent insult to everybody, but his arrogance and disregard had been too much for Jack. Jack was a broken person, and his mental deterioration by that point had already been clear evidence of the fact, but he was no pussy.

Jack had closed the distance between him and Adam in a couple of seconds, and he had grabbed Adam's green flight jacket by the collar. Adam had turned around and spit in Jack's eye and shoved him back hard. Jack had had a half-full 40oz of Olde English 800 he'd snuck into the show, and he had smashed it on Adam's bald-ass head. Adam had gone down hard. When he had, his upper body had landed on a corner of the stage. He had managed to turn around, but it had been too late. Jack had already swung his left fist. It had been on its way before Adam had turned around, so by the time Adam had faced Jack it had already practically been buried in his nose. The next three had gone straight into Adam's teeth, which had looked like they were disappearing one by one down his throat. Then Jack had buried a few elbows into Adam's temple.

It was enough already, and everybody had known it, but Jack had been in a mental frenzy. He had turned Adam around and started slamming him face-first into the stage. First, the bridge of his nose had hit the corner angle of the stage; then, it had been the forehead, opening up a disgusting gash; then it had been the mouth, wide open, being slammed into that wooden stage. People had eventually pulled him off, and Adam had left unconscious in an ambulance. It was the last anybody in the local scene had ever heard from Adam. Friendly punks had dragged Jack outside and strongly suggested he flee the scene before the cops showed up. Jack and Beth had gone back to her place. "Like he said, it wasn't much like a dream, more just a replay of that night at the show."

When Jack had woken up Beth was crying. Actually, Jack had woken up *because* Beth was crying. That had been the day that playtime had really ended. You could say that Jack had become an adult that day. You could say that if he'd learned anything, but he really hadn't. He had still been a mentally ill teenager in a man's body.

Chapter 5

Jack thought it was almost as if he had a receding leg hairline. There were strange hair patterns all over his body, and this was another example to him that God had a sense of humor. How else could you explain leg hair that refused to grow where the sock started? A practical joke worthy of humankind's creator—nothing malicious, just a reminder that's he was floating by on a cloud somewhere, pondering ways to demean lowly humans. The absence of leg hair there cast a sock-like silhouette over Jack's lower legs. God seemed to antagonize humans in much the same way that Jack had used to antagonize his G.I. Joe figures as a kid. Jack had mutilated his toys instead of cleaning his room. To Jack, God appeared to have a similar agenda for humans and planet earth.

When he was a kid, he had owned a set of tiny tools that he had saved up and bought with his allowance money. Those tools had allowed Jack to dismantle every one of his little plastic G.I. Joes and turn them into something new by swapping their body parts. He'd had a real Dr. Frankenstein's lab going in his room back then. There had been a Raleigh Tobacco can that he had taken from his grandparents' house that had stored hundreds of pieces of legs, heads, torsos, heavy-duty rubber bands from the action figures' midsections, and hundreds upon hundreds of two standard-size screws used for keeping the figures together.

In the backyard there had been a small but dignified graveyard for the fallen figures. Jack had liked blowing them up with firecrackers almost as much as he had liked playing Dr. Frankenstein. Many of his experiments had truly been Frankenstein monsters. Jack had rarely bothered matching skin tones, or even genders. Such had been the case of one poor chap with Baroness' breasted torso, Gung Ho's brawny white arms, and Roadblock's shaved black head. Sometimes, when he had run low on body parts, he'd decimated the dignity of the graveyard and picked through the fallen soldiers' graves for usable body parts. Sometimes, all he had needed was half a thigh or a lower leg piece that had survived a firecracker explosion to complete a new creation. Dr. Frankenstein would have been proud.

Jack thought it was a shame that he didn't still have G.I. Joes, considering that he had finally learned how to keep their environment clean. Jack was laughing on the inside, still looking at his weird leg hair. Maybe, he thought, God would finally learn how to clean up after his human toys. Unfortunately for the poor little toys, by the time that happens, God will have outgrown us. Jack's inside laughter turned into an actual laughing fit as he wondered what God would be into when he grew up. After Jack outgrew G.I. Joe, Jack had liked porn, alcohol, drugs, girls, and records. Jack didn't know if God had a gender, and he certainly didn't know whether God liked fucking girls or guys. Drugs and alcohol were pretty problematic, so he could see God passing on those, but records and porn were harmless. "Did God like porn and records? Of course, everybody likes porn and records."

Jack was thirty right then, it was a new millennium, and he was beyond exhausted. He'd been exhausted for years, and every day he wondered how long a person could make it like that. When it got really bad for him, he figured his mind would have to go back to its status quo level of insanity within a month or two, or else it would simply burn out. Somehow, his mind would shut down, or he'd die from a panic attack, or a heart attack. That was years ago, and Jack had lived his life in that emotional torment overdrive every single day since. He hadn't dropped dead as he'd assumed he would, and it had been like that for so long, he had actually started to believe he might just live a long life in that state. In a world full of terrifying thoughts, that one made his blood run cold.

Before Dolores had come along, he'd resolved himself to sleeping as many of the hours of the day away as he could manage. It was his solution to life; it was his escape, it was his lover, and it was his addiction. Sleeping didn't revive Jack's soul, though; it barely recharged his body. Jack had always found ways to artificially fill the hole that existed in his soul. Jack could never figure out how to do it without substances. He didn't even know if it was possible for someone like him.

Jack wondered if he'd ever even found purpose in his life with Dolores. To him, at that time, it felt like it, and right then, it felt like it was good enough for him. Jack had no models for how it was supposed to work, his life with someone. Even if he had a model, it's unlikely he would have figured it out. Jack's life was organized, on a large scale, like someone trying to assemble a jigsaw puzzle without doing the border first. That was Jack, putting together Charles Wysocki's little villages, streams, and trees with no idea where they fit in the larger picture. Dolores made Jack very happy, and by happiness he meant contentment. Maybe being content was the best Jack could ever do, but being content didn't fulfill him. Six months after Dolores and Jack moved into the new house in Puyallup, he realized two things. First, Dolores wasn't Beth. Second, there was someplace else he was supposed to be.

After that, Jack's body and mind just couldn't quit buzzing. Day after day, and week after week, it wouldn't go away. It had never been that bad before. Jack's mind became a wall of televisions with picture in picture, every channel all at once. His brain put itself into information overload. Every fear, every thought, occurred simultaneously. Terrifying thoughts flew past fifty to a hundred times an hour. The massive overload of terror occupying his mind was maddening enough, and there was no way to control or mute it. Sleep didn't do it, nor did drugs or alcohol. Dolores, sweet Dolores, try as she might, couldn't fix it, either. Before long, Jack's terror was mostly fear at the prospect of having more terrifying thoughts in the future. Jack was literally afraid of fears he might have in at some point—not the consequences of those fears coming true, but the thought of being afraid at some point in the near future.

Sometimes, after that, he had money in his pocket, but mostly he didn't. Sometimes he woke up in a motel room; most of the time it was a doorway, or a box, a newspaper bin, or under a bridge. Sometimes, he woke up in four-point restraints in a rubber room.

He fell out of the world. He got lost, and he stayed lost to everyone for years. During lucid interludes in the bipolar, obsessive compulsive, anxious, depressed madness that had finally over-whelmed Jack's life, he was struck with the feeling that he was completely alone. He could have found someone to help him. He could have found a psychiatric facility, a girlfriend, or even just a friend. But his particular blend of afflictions ensured that anyone that might help could never do more than misdiagnose, misunderstand, or pity his plight. That was what really hurt Jack, those years. He was certifiably nuts, and he hated but accepted that fact, but not having one other human being that could really understand his torment was unbearable.

Prior to that period, Jack had given up on himself time and time again, but there had always been some sustaining force keeping him afloat. Sometimes, it had been Jack's crew, or Dolores, or Beth, or his mom. Sometimes, it had just been simple spite, and an ingrained need to prove all those people who had looked down their nose at him wrong. In every instance, the will to survive was simply a distraction from the real problem, the problem of being Jack.

Conversely, self-destructing was just a distraction as well. Neither distraction made his mind quiet or his body stop working. Nothing did. Jack's mind was wired to go bad right away, but his body was wired to keep living for a long time. The end result was always the same: every day, Jack kept waking up. His mind wouldn't give him a moment's peace, no matter how hard he beat it with substances, and his body wouldn't stop living, no matter how hard he beat it with substances. He was stuck, alive, and alone.

Nobody likes self-pity in a character; people want drama and somebody to root for. Sad stories could leave a lasting impression, though. *1984* gives one the bleakest, dystopian views imaginable, but the last line punched you in the gut like a real fist punching you in the gut. An actual punch to the gut went away after a few minutes, but the end of *1984* hurt years later. Sad could work, but self-pity never played well, never.

Jack gave up during that time. He never loved Big Brother, but he was defeated just the same. No human could've remained intact under that strain he was under, and he never pitied himself. He hated his circumstances, was resentful and angry at the hand life had dealt him, but never really stopped trying to get up again. It was futile, of course, and the older he got, the more he realized that he was a fly trying to escape from a closed window. How many flies have you found lying in the crook of a sliding window? There they lie, crusty and dry, only the slightest pressure from a human finger needed to turn those little bodies into a thousand tiny twigs of exoskeleton. The window was solid. That simplest observation of any person was completely lost on the fly. The fly would smash its head against the glass, searching for an open spot you knew didn't exist, until it died. It was cruel to watch the fly without opening the window; it was sadistic to enjoy watching the fly without opening the window. The futility of the fly's situation was obvious and tragic. You might as well have asked a child to flip a fire engine.

Jack was in a bad state then, but he didn't pity himself. He just kept banging his head into the glass, looking, against all odds, for the open spot in the window. Eventually, I learned to pity him, but he didn't pity himself. In any case, for those of us watching his life, it went from unwatchable to unbearable.

Seeing it was unbearable, but living it must have been excruciating. It was four years, give or take, and most people who knew Jack secretly hoped he would find the courage to end his own life, or overdose, or get hit by a bus. Most were ashamed to say it, but Jack's death would have alleviated the guilt of many that cared about him. People are allowed to feel like that. Caring for an ill person takes its toll on the loved ones, too. Everybody suffers. Of course, there's shame attached to any such thought, but it exists nonetheless.

Chapter 6

When a person starts off his mental break by stealing his girlfriend's Volkswagen bug and driving it to Utah for some fresh air, the story probably doesn't get better from there. That's how Jack got started. Sounds ridiculous, doesn't it? It had always been something ridiculous, but it never seemed so to him. It had seemed like the logical next step in a sequence of events, or an imperative. That time, it had been nothing less than that, an imperative. There was a city in the mountains where thousands of unspoiled Mormon college girls resided, a place where there was clean mountain air.

Provo, Utah, that was the destination. As he pulled out of the 7-11 parking lot, forty ounces of Olde English 800 in hand, cigarette in mouth, and prescribed medications nowhere to be found, Jack imagined his future life. That clean air, and pure-minded Mormon college girls, that was the ticket. It was the thing that was finally going to lead him to the clean living. In Provo, he'd find work chopping wood or cleaning mountain cabins. He wasn't really sure, but chopping wood and cleaning mountain cabins were the only occupations his somewhat ignorant brain could come up with.

He figured that, in his free time, he'd ski for free, since he'd work at one of the ski resorts. In the spring, he'd come down from the resort into the college town. Those college girls would love him. He'd be in great shape from all the wood chopping and cabin cleaning. He wouldn't smoke or drink. Plus, he'd have a great 4x4. It was fall again, which, in Washington, just meant nine straight months of rain and early sunsets, the dark wet. But in Utah, it meant nine months of skiing and cabin parties.

Dolores' car always smelled both abandoned and lived in at the same time. Jack wondered if Volkswagen was thinking about a rainy climate when they had designed it, because, whenever it rained, it seemed like every surface on the inside of the car was constantly wet. In western Washington, that was a bad thing. Everything outside was already constantly wet at that time of year, and importing that to the inside of a tiny tin can of a car made existing in it miserable. Those fake leather seats, wet. The tiny little dashboard, wet. The gross little gearshift boot popping out of the floor, wet. The inside of that flat-as-a-board little windshield, wet. The mushy, carpeted floorboard mats, squishy and wet. The whole car smelled wet, like mildew and old sweat simultaneously. Sometimes it smelled like an old coat. Most of the time, it smelled like exhaust and gas.

Jack's spit was starting to take on the consistency of the malt liquor he was drinking. The taste was rank, but Jack barely noticed it anymore. Sometimes he caught a hint of it when he opened the first one and took a drink, and when that happened, he couldn't help but think he was drinking someone's distilled body odor. It was worth it, though. Soon, Jack's lips would start tingling, and he'd get butterflies in his stomach that let him know the booze was starting to have an effect. He hadn't drunk in a while, and he got that feeling in his stomach, that feeling like he had a fart that wouldn't come out. It was that bloated, gaseous feeling that just made you laugh instead of fart. If you didn't know it was just alcohol pooling and expanding in your stomach, you might be inclined to go sit on a toilet somewhere and wait for the fart to come out.

Jack was a well-orientated drunk, and had great balance, too. One time, at a DOA show, he was standing next to the stage all of two feet from the pit, and this guy had torpedoed out at him like someone had shot him out of a slingshot. Jack had done one of those falls, like in a Looney Tunes episode, where he was completely horizontal in the air before he slammed straight down on his back, but he had turned the beer cup in his hand ninety degrees into an upright position to keep it from spilling. After that, some people in the crowd had picked him up and put him on his feet, and as they had, he had turned the cup ninety degrees back again so the beer didn't spill. One of them had said, "How'd you do that?" Jack had said, "Do what?" "You didn't spill your beer." Jack hadn't even been aware he'd done it.

It was all just some reflex and reaction super-power. Jack was all reflex and reaction, and he needed it. God gave the reflex and reaction su-perpower to the Irish and house cats. Jack was one of those things. Anyhow, neither the Irish nor house cats could survive without it, and no one was sure why cats had it at all. After all, nobody liked cats anyway. Irish people were another story. Everybody loved the Irish. The English were so in love with the Irish they'd been trying to fuck them for thousands of years. One way or the other, that reflex and reaction superpower ensured that house cats and Irish people survived situations that would otherwise be fatal. It was true; you could watch a cat fall out of a window and somehow land safely on the limb of a nearby tree.

One time, a guy had hit Jack so hard he was literally out cold on his feet. Instead of collapsing,

Jack had lurched toward the guy, fish hooked him, and then fallen down. On the way down, the guy had hit his temple on the hood of the car that was behind him. Jack had hit the ground, but the impact had actually woken him up. The other guy had been concussed and hadn't gotten up for several minutes. Jack had never landed a single punch, but he had been up on his feet, and the other guy had been out cold on the pavement.

Whenever he was driving, the superpower worked double. Jack woke up at the steering wheel a lot. Usually, the car was in motion, and often Jack was only a few seconds from certain death. It was rarely two tons of steel a hundred miles an hour, but scary nonetheless. At no point did Jack wear a seatbelt, ever. On that occasion, in Dolores' bug, Jack woke up to see a large tree coming at him. Jack had passed out, and he was actually coming at the tree doing about sixty. The road ahead curved sharp to the left. It was too late for the brakes, and bracing for impact seemed like his only choice. Instead, Jack somehow managed to clip a raised center median strip with the left front wheel, and it spun the bug one hundred and eighty degrees.

He'd put the bug in neutral, so he was still travelling about twenty miles per hour, only backwards, when the rear bumper hit the tree, slamming Jack rearward into his seat. Jack began cursing his luck until he realized that, without his seat belt on, and doing sixty, he likely would have been ejected from the bug and died on the ground shortly thereafter. Even if he'd had his seat belt on, the bug would have been totaled, and he would have been in the middle of nowhere with no transportation whatsoever. As it was, he had some minor discomfort, and a dented rear bumper. "Thank you very fuckin' much, reflex and reaction superpower gods."

He figured the alignment wouldn't be totally right after that, but it hadn't been totally right before that. The bug had stalled during the collision, so Jack pushed the clutch in and tried the ignition. The engine started back up, and after piloting it out of the brush and back onto the dark forest road, the steering seemed no worse for the wear. Jack couldn't remember anything for at least two hours preceding the tree collision. It was definitely time to check the map and compass.

All Jack needed to go anywhere in the world was a map and a compass. It was a handy skill to have before anyone could go anywhere simply because they had navigation on a smartphone. Laurence and Jack had both been in the Boy Scouts. Jack's dad had been their scoutmaster. He had taught Laurence and Jack how to read maps and use a compass when they were kids. Their dad was a Vietnam vet, and he had run their Boy Scout troop like it was his platoon in the jungles outside of Huế City. Jack was sure his dad had thought he was a flake, undisciplined and weak-willed. Jack actually appreciated skills like the ability to navigate from one place to another. In reality, Jack's dad had taught Laurence things, and Jack had just happened to be around. Jack hadn't realized that he was an afterthought to his dad when he was young, but he was fully aware of the fact by the time he was grown.

It took about fifteen or twenty minutes, but Jack finally found an ampm near Caldwell, Idaho. In his blackout, it appeared that Jack had meandered his way down I-84 through at least a couple hundred miles of rural Oregon and into Idaho. Sometime after he'd crossed into Idaho, he'd gotten off the interstate and onto Idaho State Route 95. Out there was where he had hit the tree. Once he'd gotten back on I-84, finding more beer and gas was pretty simple. There were no hunger pangs, but Jack suspected he should eat anyway. He didn't. Jack actually liked the rubbery ampm hamburgers, but this was not an eating day. He figured he'd eat the next day, after he'd made it to Provo.

Caldwell was by no means a metropolis, but it was big enough to support one or two twenty-four-hour gas stations. It was quiet at night, and, based on the quaint nature of Main Street, Jack supposed the city was pretty quiet during the day, too. There was probably a kegger on Saturday night down under the bridge that crossed Indian Creek, but most of the automobiles around there were 1970s GMC, Ford, or Chevy pickups, all equipped with rifle racks. Most of those racks had at least one rifle on them; some had two or three. The Fords seemed the most heavily armed, the Chevys the least, and the GMCs had plenty of rifles, just not as many as the Fords. One rack Jack saw had a compound bow. It was in a GMC. Odd bunch the GMC crowd, he mumbled out loud. He didn't know why, but when he went to new places, Jack always tried to imagine living there. Caldwell seemed like a fine place. It seemed like a place where you could shoot holes in the empty keg after the party down by the river. It was definitely a place where you could hear country music at the bar and hook up with a Treasure Valley farmgirl in a barn later that night. All of that actually sounded pretty fun, and for a moment Jack considered sticking around for a day or two. He didn't. He knew that once he stopped, he'd probably be stopped for a while. No farmgirls for Jack. Caldwell was only going to be a pit stop. Besides, he didn't have a trucker hat or a Stetson, and if he was going to hang around Caldwell, he'd need one or the other. The truck and rifle rack were negotiable, but the hat was mandatory.

It had been a while since he had peed. It had

been a while since he had stood up. When you sat and drove for a long time, you could develop some serious bladder control. As long as you didn't move much, you could drive a hundred miles on a full bladder. At least, Jack could. Unfortunately, not stopping to pee meant not standing up. Jack had been drinking the whole drive, or at least he assumed he had. Blackouts had never stopped him from drinking in the past, so why would they now? Jack had it on good authority from practically every person he'd ever been close to that not only did Jack continue to drink in blackouts, but he would get up, go to the store or a bar, purchase more alcohol, and keep drinking.

Jack stepped out of the bug, stood up straight to stretch, and immediately grabbed the open car door. The tunnel vision had come over him quick. The combination of alcohol and whiplash from his earlier accident almost put him on the pavement. In typical Jack fashion, he grabbed the door handle and reclaimed control of one leg on the way down. For a second, he balanced on that one leg while the other pointed straight out behind him. His left hand held the door handle for dear life, and his nose was no more than three inches from the ground. He didn't know how to stand up from that position, but he looked like a figure skater in the camel position. Eventually, he just bent the knee of the leg he was balancing on and slowly lowered himself onto the pavement.

Jack was already out of sorts, even for him, and the inside of the ampm didn't help. ampms are the emergency rooms of convenience stores. Everything is bright white, or some hideous neon orange or purple. There are bright lines painted on the gleaming white tiles, pointing you to where things are. Ten seconds of exposure to the harsh fluorescent lights alone made Jack's eyes hurt. The hamburgers and hot dogs were all sterile in their aluminum foil packaging. Sterile convenience was a thing.

All ampms were ten percent too much of everything. Ten percent too much light. Ten percent too much bright white walls. Ten percent too glossy floor tiles. It was like it was designed by someone who'd read books about Americans but had never been to America. Even the human behind the counter was ten percent too much.

This particular human was in his early twenties. Somehow, his creator had crammed all the worst things about being an adolescent and young man into this one sad creature. He had terrible acne and a patchy beard. Instead of shaving, he had just let the whiskers grow over the pimples. He was too skinny and too short. Usually, people were one or the other. His glasses were too small, but his lenses were way too thick. Was he human? Was he a facsimile of a human? Jack didn't want to stick around to find out. He asked for a pack of Marlboro Reds in a box, paid for his beer and smokes, and got the fuck out of there. When he walked in there, Jack had been worried the guy would sweat him about almost falling outside. By the time he left, he was just glad the guy hadn't beamed him up to his mothership.

Jack already had that new 40oz of 8 ball a third empty as the gas filled the bug. He was staring at the map and smoking a Marlboro Red when he started thinking about his dad again. The Cockney Rejects' cassette was playing "Beginning of the End" for at least the twelfth time on this trip.

Jack may have been an afterthought to his dad, but he had never realized that, despite outward appearances, Jack had easily absorbed and utilized more of what his dad had taught them than Laurence ever had. Jack saw the front passenger tire sagging and decided to fill it up before he left. Jack doubted Laurence could have even changed that tire, much less taken apart the front suspension and replaced the shocks that had just taken a beating when he had hit that median back there. Jack could. He had watched his dad do it one time. After that, Jack had started taking everything apart just to see if he could put it back together. Once he had started driving, the cars he could afford to own had routinely been in such poor shape that he had become a fairly skilled backyard mechanic. As for navigation, Laurence had gotten lost in the woods by their house growing up; he would certainly have been no help on a rural state route highway.

Chapter 7

Jack felt sorry for people that should have felt sorry for him. That is, Jack felt sad when he looked at people with low-paying jobs, crappy apartments, and shitty cars. Jack had no job, a cheap motel room, and a stolen car. When Jack made it to Provo, he immediately started feeling sorry for all the locals.

Jack turned thirty during his first week in Utah, and in a few more weeks the millennium would end. The prophetic Cockney Rejects tape was still playing, the beginning of the end indeed. People had been talking about all the computers crashing when their clocks rolled over to the new millennium. Y2K was the buzzword of the season. Jack didn't worry much about it. In reality, he thought a world without an electronic infrastructure could be good for him. He'd failed to excel in the world up to that point, but a chaotic mind, he thought, might thrive in a chaotic world. He was probably right. The ambitions of the insane always seemed to thrive in a vacuum of order. Jack's problem was that he kept trying to assimilate into polite society. He'd bottom out, then eventually try to assimilate again. If he rejected a rules-based structure altogether, he'd probably be much happier.

Provo didn't live up to the wood-chopping, clean living paradise, he'd made it out to be in his head. He settled into a place ironically named the Six Star Motel. It was ironic because of the reality of the place, but also because there was no such thing as a five-star motel, much less a six-star one. After driving around for three hours, it was the only motel he could find with a weekly rate. One hundred and ten dollars a week. He had about five hundred in his bank account, so he figured he could survive for about a month if he quit eating food altogether and only drank cheap beer on the weekends. Cigarettes, however, were a daily necessity. The plan sounded solid; plenty of time to find a job and apartment.

It turned out that living in a garbage motel was actually not very cheap. In fact, on a day-to-day basis, it was a lot more expensive than an apartment. After he'd been in town for a couple of days, he started buying the Daily Herald at the 7-Eleven up the street. There really wasn't much to do at the Six Star Motel most of the time, and reading the paper killed a large portion of the afternoon. It turned out that Jack could have rented a studio apartment for less than two hundred and fifty dollars a month. Jack intended to stop drinking during the week, but instead he just started buying cases of Rainier at the 7-Eleven. The convenience stores couldn't sell strong beer, wine, or booze, so he had to resort to drinking more beer.

Jack didn't know it when he arrived, but the strongest beer convenience stores could sell were only 3.2% alcohol. The 7-Eleven clerk tried to explain something about the difference between alcohol by weight and alcohol by volume, but Jack didn't really track it. All he knew was that his Olde English 40s still tasted like shit but barely got him drunk. He loved Olde English, but mainly because of its effect. It had always tasted like shit, and now the State of Utah had taken away its main redeeming quality. That was why Jack switched to Rainier. Like Olde English, Rainier was cheap, but at least it tasted alright. It was less portable, since you had to buy a case of it to get drunk, but Jack adjusted. There was a state-run liquor store within walking distance where he could get real booze, but the 7-Eleven clerk told Jack that off-duty cops worked at those places, so he steered clear.

There was no motel lobby at the Six Star, just a rusted dumpster out front that was full of old beer bottles. Jack knew it was full of beer bottles because he could see them in the blinding Provo daylight, and because when he threw his beer bottles in, all he heard was glass breaking. The manager's office window was practically on the city sidewalk, and it had a great view of the street, but effectively no view of what was going on in, or immediately outside, the motel rooms. And there was a lot going on both in and outside those rooms.

Every room had an exterior entrance and a bathroom equipped with an ample-sized window located at the rear of the room. The entrance to the parking lot was tight, as the motel sat on the south side of the lot, and a Chinese restaurant butted up against the Six Star's lot to the north. The whole place seemed designed to shield the anonymity of those inside the rooms while allowing the front office plenty of time to see problems like inbound cops. The position of the office also gave plausible deniability to the manager, as he or she could see very little of what was going on inside. Even the bathroom windows seemed intentionally placed to allow people to smuggle their friends in for parties.

The rooms themselves were adequate. The brown shag carpet masked what was surely years of beer and blood stains and who knew what else. The walls were off-white enough not to completely give away their actual level of dinginess. There were sheets on the bed—just sheets, no comforter, which didn't bother Jack. They seemed clean enough, and to

Jack "clean enough" just meant they didn't smell like the cooch of the last prostitute to have slept or worked in the room. There were roaches, though. He noticed a few behind the TV, and some more under the minifridge where he kept the Rainier.

The bathroom was nice, though. It was turf-green Formica on the countertops. It was actually turf-green throughout: the sink, the shower, and the floor. When Jack took a dump, he had a great view of the exposed particle board beneath the chipped veneer of the Formica. The first time he noticed this, he also noticed that the particle board beneath the veneer was waterlogged, and he wondered what varieties of mold must have spawned in a near-completely encased piece of waterlogged particle board. He assumed he would see a roach crawl out of the open space between that waterlogged particle board and warped Formica, but it never happened. Then Jack got up, flushed, and looked in the bathroom sink, where he immediately saw a roach crawling into the drain. "I fuckin' knew there had to be one in here! Now shit makes sense again."

It was miraculous to Jack that he'd found the one place in that hive of Mormonism where vice flourished unencumbered. "As far as I can tell, this motel is hooker central, and the only place in Provo to score any blow at all." Nothing about the Six Star was helping Jack realize his goal of good, clean living. The Rockies literally surrounded the city. If Jack had to guess, he'd have said the base of some of them started three blocks west of the Six Star, but sitting and drinking in the lawn chair in the vacant lot behind the Six Star was the closest he ever got to the mountains.

In addition, there were two prostitutes, Rosa and Simone, that both lived and worked out of the Six Star, and Jack had blown large portions of the little money he had fucking them.

Rosa was a voluptuous Mexican woman, about thirty: big breasts, wide hips, full lips, really sexy. She drank a lot as well, so Jack liked hanging around with her. Plus, she only charged him for actual sheet time; drinking and hanging out was free. Sometimes, free was too high a price even for Jack. Rosa blacked out more easily than Jack when she drank, and when she did, she would either start crying uncontrollably or scream and throw things.

If you looked closely, it was apparent that most things in Rosa's room had been the target of her drunken rage at one time or another. The glass of the TV screen was cracked. The blinds were destroyed and discarded on the floor beneath the window. The shower curtain rod had obviously been torn down and rehung poorly. There were holes in all the walls, and if you walked around her room in bare feet you were sure to step on tiny shards of glass, the too-small-to-pick-up, remnants of unlucky beer bottles. They were embedded everywhere, and Jack learned to keep his shoes on in Rosa's room. That is, unless it was sheet time. Rosa was a good time, and she had a good time. She always had friends and customers coming by. Jack had to clear the room in favor of paying customers many times during the few weeks he was there.

Simone, which he doubted was her real name, was less sexy, and more tragic. She was blond and skinny, heroin chic. She had dark circles under her eyes, dried-out lips, and a generally unhealthy appearance. Jack was sure the thigh-high stockings she wore while she was working only stayed up because they were attached to those straps on the garter belt. Rosa's legs needed no straps; her shapely legs were all that she needed to keep her stockings up.

Simone was a cokehead; he knew that much because whenever he came to her room, she was snorting it, and because Jack scored blow off her a few times. She was also probably a junkie, because Jack could see collapsed veins on both arms, and when she took her stockings off, she had what appeared to be fresh track marks on the tops of both feet. If she was a junkie, she didn't like talking about it. Worst of all, once you entered her room, she was on the clock. She didn't like to hang out and drink, and Jack almost never saw other customers come to her room. Jack certainly never saw anyone that looked like a friend come by. They found her dead in her room a week before Jack left town. He never found out for sure, but he knew it was a heroin overdose.

Jack doubted it was an accident.Simone seemed like the sort of girl that either used the last of her money to overdose on purpose, or slammed a hit she suspected was too much for her to handle with careless disregard for the consequences.

Nobody came for her things. Jack and Rosa heard of no memorial. Jack suspected Simone had just been cremated, and after that her ashes had just been placed on a shelf somewhere in a county coroner's office. Jack had never seen one, but he knew there was a shelf like that where Jane and Jack Doe sat alongside all the people with real names but no friends or family to claim them. It was ironic, Simone spent her life all alone, and now she was surrounded by the remains of others, and those others were people who likely spent their lives all alone. Loners that they were, they probably would have preferred separate shelves, but Jack just knew they were all crammed together on one shelf.

Jack parked the bug down the street from the Six Star. About a week after he started staying there, it was towed. It was stolen, so he didn't want it at the motel or associated with him at all. He essentially abandoned it, but he kept an eye on it, hoping it would make its way back to Dolores. He never found out if it did, but he left a note in the glovebox that read:

"Hey Dolores, if you never got this bug back, I'm sorry and I owe you one 1972 Volkswagen Beetle, color orange. If that's the case, I'll have to apologize again, because if you never get it back, you will not have seen this note. If you did get it back, I assume I owe you some towing and inconvenience fees. Plus, there's a new dent on the back bumper and the alignment might be a little out. I'll settle up with you about those later when I have some cash. Anyway, like I said, I'm sorry about all this, and I'm sorry about a lot of other things too. Love Jack."

During a period where he was more or less sane for a couple of days, Jack applied for and, amazingly, got a job at the Taco Bell across the 189 highway from the BYU campus. It was maybe two miles from the Six Star, but Jack didn't mind the walk. Walking was the only exercise he'd gotten since arriving in Utah. All that walking was probably the only thing that kept him physically functional during that period. His Utah experience had consisted of walking to and from the 7-Eleven, which was not quite a mile from the Six Star. Now, working at the Taco Bell, he would more than double that.

In addition, he was eating every day again. He was able to eat at work for free, and that became his daily sustenance. Technically, he was supposed to pay for food he took home, but the night shift manager let him take whatever he wanted. Jack never ate after work, because if he filled his stomach up with food, he couldn't get drunk. He still took food back to the Six Star, though. Sometimes, it would just sit on the table in his room until the next morning, when he would throw it out. Most of the time, he'd go over to Rosa's room with his beers and the food from work.

Pretty much every night after Simone died up until Jack left town, he headed over to Rosa's room with a bag full of burritos and tacos. There were only four channels on the TV, so they would usually watch documentaries on PBS. At the beginning of that last week, Rosa started cuddling with Jack on the bed for no apparent reason. Before long, they were fucking like normal people instead of fucking for money. Jack still had to split when her pager went off. The pager meant a paying customer, and a girl had to make a living, after all, but even Jack had to admit that, for all intents and purposes, Rosa was his girlfriend at that point.

Taco Bell was actually a good place for a mentally ill alcoholic to work. All fast-food places have a strong odor about them, but that seemed especially so at Taco Bell. The smell of refried beans and odd-smelling meats covered up much of the booze aroma that permeated from Jack's pores. Plus, since there were always a couple of other employees that were clearly losing at the game of life, Jack's constant hangover-induced, diminished work performance seemed almost quaint by comparison. It didn't go unnoticed, but almost.

One of his fellow employees was a girl named Megan. Megan's husband got drunk nightly. She worked the drive-thru, mostly, but when she had a fat lip, Thomas, the shift manager, would put her on the back food line making orders. Megan's husband typically used her for a punching bag for ten minutes before using her as a fuck doll. The punching bag part was obvious to anybody that saw her face. Jack found out about the rapes one especially bad day when he was out by the dumpster smoking. Megan and her husband were sitting in his exhausted-looking Honda Civic. It sounded like he was trying to apologize for the previous night's violence when Megan screamed: "But it doesn't matter when you fucking rape me, does it?" She apologized to Jack that he'd had to hear that, but he was pretty sure that she had wanted him to.

Megan was a Pomeranian with glasses—cute, but stupid. She'd worked at that Taco Bell for over two years but struggled with aspects of the job that Jack mastered on his second day. The fact that she was going nowhere and never would made her life sad. The fact that she had two kids that almost surely glued her to that abusive husband for life made her life a tragedy.

Peter, the methhead, actually trained Jack. Peter missed work three times in the two-and-a-half weeks Jack worked at that Taco Bell, yet he was still somehow considered a model employee. Usually, the most exciting part of Jack's morning was seeing what had happened to Peter the night before. Peter only slept once or twice a week, so what had happened the night before, to Peter, was really just what he had done before work.

The manager, Jeff, was a compulsive sex addict and pedophile, and despite being married, he attempted to fuck all the underage girls that worked there. In that endeavor, he was rarely successful, but Jack had certainly seen him coming out of Simone's room at the Six Star. That is, before Simone had died.

The assistant manager, Hannah, on the other hand, fucked all the sixteen-year-old guys that worked there, so Jack guessed she was sort of a pedophile, too. She was probably in her late twenties, but she seemed a lot older. She had pale, freckled skin and curly red hair. She really wasn't much to look at, but her jiggly tits were always spilling out of her balconette bra, which was always spilling out of her work shirt because she didn't button the top three buttons of it. In any other context, she wouldn't have gotten a second look from Jack, but standing next to her tits all day on the food line had broken Jack down, and he'd started wishing he was sixteen. Once, Jack asked her if he could put the meat in her taco. "No, that's not how I said it. I asked if I could stuff her taco. She gave me a blank stare, and I was like, you know what I'm talkin' 'bout. She was like, 'No, I got it.' Anyway, then she just went on foldin' burritos. Clearly, she only liked teenage boys."

This seventeen-year-old kid named Randy worked there, too. He was the only normal one in the whole place. Well, he was normal by Provo standards. He went to church, got good grades at school, and was going to college in the fall. He didn't smoke or get high, and only got drunk with his friends at the occasional party. He was the only underage guy there that hadn't let Hannah bust his cherry.

It wasn't much of a fresh start, but Jack had a job and a roof over his head. Even in a crowd of addicts, molesters, and battered women, Jack sunk to the lowest common denominator. It lasted for about two and a half weeks before it all came crashing down on him again.

Taco Bell was keeping him nourished. Prior to working at Taco Bell, he had only eaten a few times a week. At least when he worked around food, he ate every day. Jack could only get four-hour shifts, but he figured out that what he made at Taco Bell would just barely pay for his room, beer, and smokes.

Knowing that he'd be able to cover the necessities should have been a great relief to him, but he just couldn't keep from fucking up. Jack's cash register was always short, and not just because he was stealing. It was mostly just sloppy cash handling. He only stole a few bucks a day, and that was just when he pocketed orders where a person paid with exact change. Everything else he did was wrong too, though. He was constantly late, not only for his shifts but also coming back from breaks and lunch. His hygiene was an issue, too. He washed his uniform in the bathroom sink of his room, but not very often. In addition, Jack rarely shaved more than once a week, and he smelled like a brewery even on the rare occasions when he showered. The writing was on the wall, so on payday, Jack took his check to the bank during his lunch and never went back. He never went back to drop off his uniform. He never went back to say goodbye to anyone.

He was nearly a week back on rent at the Six Star when he bolted. It surprised Jack that the manager didn't stop Jack and ask him about rent every time she saw him walk by the office. Jack knew the manager couldn't possibly be so blissfully ignorant to believe that he was going to pay that back rent. Did she even think Jack was capable of making good on that rent? Jack figured the manager must be used to derelicts trying to welch on the rent. Maybe she knew Jack wasn't going to pay, or maybe she just didn't care. It annoyed Jack that he couldn't figure out what that motel manager intended to do to get the rent from him, but whatever the case was, it was surely no surprise when Jack just wasn't there one day.

It may have come as a surprise to Rosa that he wasn't there, but he'd never know. He never said goodbye. He didn't even slip a letter under her door. He felt bad, but convinced himself she wouldn't even miss him. "She's so wasted most of the time, she probably don't even notice I ain't there. Just like everythin' else in life, Utah ain't shit to me. Rosa was nice, but oh well. She was a big girl. I'm sure she was fine. It was all just a big fuckin' joke, and I couldn't care less about any of it. Lost some shitty job, no place to go, no semblance of sanity left, and then I just move along leavin' nothin' good behind. Same old shit, different fuckin' day."

If life was that simple to Jack, he'd have been a happier person, but it wasn't. Jack was no desperado, humping and pillaging his way through the old west. Jack incurred invisible scars on his soul every time this happened. His mental illnesses, and the reactionary impulsive actions they caused, ensured he would leave people in the cold, and the innate humanity he lacked the ability to discard ensured he would suffer as a result of those very actions.

Jack's last paycheck didn't buy much, but it didn't need to. What it did get him was a Greyhound ticket back to T-town, a decent meal, a couple fifths of whiskey, and five packs of cigarettes. That was it, almost down to the penny. Generally, he didn't care much for whiskey. Jack was a beer drinker, and more specifically malt liquor drinker, but under the circumstances he had to make do. Drinking on the bus without somebody saying something to the bus driver was hard enough with a bottle of whiskey. It was almost impossible with a paper sack full of 40oz bottles of Olde English 800 crammed in under the seat, or a few cases of Rainier stuffed into the overhead compartment. His alcohol for this trip had to be compact, so whiskey it was. Besides, the bus didn't make a lot of stops at the corner store on the way back to Tacoma, so purchasing more alcohol on the way was not really an option. And drinking whiskey instead of beer meant fewer trips to that rank little pisser in the back of the bus.

On top of all that, if he hadn't spent all his money on alcohol and cigarettes right away, he might have been tempted to buy something foolish, like food. To him, it was beyond debate that booze and cigarettes were much more important than food. Alcohol would continue to hold its lead in Jack's hierarchy of priorities for some time to come.

Chapter 8

I nterlude. People really do have a good side and a bad one most of the time. You hear it all the time. "Photograph my good side." All the scars Jack had were on the right side of his body. Even the patchy part of his beard was on the right side. He couldn't even grow a decent sideburn on the right side. He didn't like people lingering around his right side.

Jack lingered around the Greyhound station in downtown Tacoma for a couple of hours. He wasn't sure of his next move. Somehow, he had figured his next move would become clear once he stepped off the bus. It didn't, so he sat in the bus station lobby staring blankly into the powerless screens of one of those little TVs they used to attach to the arms of the lobby chairs. He had no money to turn it on, so he just stared intently into it, hoping the employees would conclude that he was waiting for a departing bus. They didn't. They knew he was just loitering.

Nobody was there to meet him. Nobody knew he was there. He hadn't bothered to inform anyone of his impending arrival. Of course, nobody was there. Jack was still disappointed, as though people should have intuited his early morning arrival. "At least nobody had missed me," Jack muttered to himself. Right then, there was a knock on the station's front window. The knocker was Walter, his old roommate from the halfway house where Jack had stayed briefly before he met Dolores.

Walter wanted to know why Jack hadn't been home lately. Jack told him that he hadn't lived at the halfway house for a couple of years. Walter had some smokes and five dollars. Jack couldn't remember Walter ever having cigarettes of his own or even one dollar, much less five. He took the cigarette Walter offered him and asked him if he could borrow a quarter for the phone. Walter asked Jack if he was hungry, and since he'd only been out of booze for about eight hours, Jack was both in early withdrawal and, oddly enough, sort of hungry. They trudged up the 9th Street hill in the pissing rain to the McDonald's by the county jail, where Walter bought him two cheeseburgers and asked him again why he hadn't been home lately. Jack was barely able to keep one cheeseburger down, so Walter finished off the other one.

He hadn't seen Walter in two years, but Walter's life story of descent into lunacy was an intrusive thought that had never really left Jack. Sometimes, it went to sleep for a while, but it always woke up, and when it did, Jack's heart palpitated and beads of sweat emerged from the pores of his body with amazing efficiency. Jack's terror was pure and potent, one hundred and eighty proof, and each occurrence of it constituted a discrete PTSD event for him. Jack wondered for a minute how his PTSD compared to Walter's, and that thought triggered another PTSD event for him.

Back when he had lived at the halfway house, Jack was scared he would someday turn into Walter. Sitting at the McDonald's, he started to wonder if turning into Walter was actually preferrable. Walter was right where he had been two years ago and seemingly no worse for wear. As far as Jack could tell, Walter was barely aware of the passage of time at all. Jack was acutely aware of every little thing that had ever transpired. Every single day was a year to him, and every one of those yearlong days was a walk up a muddy mountain trail. Now, Jack cursed God for not turning him into Walter more quickly.

Jack called Todd to see about crashing on his couch for a little while. The next morning, he made a trip to the DSHS office to get emergency food stamps. While he was there, he filled out the forms to get back on GAU.

He framed it to people as a life reboot, but it was

just another defeat. Every couple of years, it happened to him. Jack had been dancing dangerously close to involuntary commitment since that night he had left for Utah, and now he experienced the foreboding that preceded the actual commitment. He knew that within a short period, the fear and apprehension would all but melt away, and that by the time it happened, he'd almost welcome it. He always did. Eventually, his minute-to-minute existence would scare him into a desire for the structure that only the removal of personal autonomy could guarantee. He wondered if Beth would still be there all these years later. He wasn't ready to go quite yet, but soon.

Chapter 9

Something had happened at those bikers' place the night of Jack's going-away party. He hadn't known it at the time, but it really had been his going-away party. To that day, Jack couldn't tell you what had happened for sure. Like much of his life, it had happened in a blackout. As with any other blackout, Jack never fully or even partially recollected what had happened that night. He didn't remember what had happened, but he did know a couple of things. He had woken up in Beth's bed covered in blood. He knew that. Also, he hadn't been cut anywhere, so the blood hadn't been his. He knew that, too.

This would be a great pivot point. The part in the story where Jack put all the pieces of the puzzle together and began to live a meaningful life. The part where he faced the music, and ultimately became a better person for it. I, your narrator, and Jack's greatest fan, would like to tell you that story, but that's not Jack's story. Your narrator owes Jack, not the reader, and Jack deserves to have his story told the way it happened. Jack's is a cautionary tale, yes, but Jack is a human being, not a device to make the reader feel better.

Waking up like that was a hard feeling to describe. Jack had woken up covered in blood a hundred times, but when it had happened before it had always been his blood. He'd lumbered into the bathroom, and upon closer examination had always found something like a laceration on his hand, arm, or foot. He'd certainly found broken, bloody 40oz bottles around after waking up with blood on him, and so there had never been much of a mystery to solve. He had fallen with a bottle and sliced his hand or arm. He had walked on a broken bottle he'd forgotten about and sliced up his foot. Going to bed with a wound gushing rather than dressing it was a very Jack thing to do. In any case, in the past, bloody sheets had always been pretty easily explained, but not then. And Beth had certainly never woken up in a blood-drenched bed before.

Beth had been pretty freaked out, obviously. Her reaction had been that of a person who had never woken up with the soft sole of her foot sliced through to the big toe's tendon. She certainly had not been happy about the state of the sheets. She hadn't screamed, though. She was a nurse, after all, but she had been pretty scared and confused. Of course, her first reaction had been that Jack had bled to death in bed, so she had woken him up immediately.

Jack had had a pretty clear mind, which in and of itself had surprised him. He had felt pretty banged up, but he had been able to tell, even without a self-examination, that he wasn't cut. Beth's sheets had blue and white zig-zag stripes, and Jack had thought the pools of red blood actually gave the sheets a bit of a patriotic appeal. With the backdrop of Beth's antique iron-frame bed, the scene had been a nice little slice of Americana. Jack imagined that a painting of the two of them staring at the bloody bed would have made a handsome addition to some art gallery or museum. It could be titled something like *Patriotism and Valor at Home*.

Beth had begun questioning Jack about what had happened. Jack had been as polite as possible under the circumstances, but also annoyed. She had to know that he had been blacked out. Asking him what had happened wasn't going to make an answer magically appear. He was used to blackout mysteries, and he had periodically had some luck solving them. He was more interested in beginning the process of retracing his steps.

Waking up not knowing what happened was always scary, but that day it had been terrifying. This was different. Most of the time, he had woken afraid something bad happened, even though there was really no indication that anything had. That day, he knew something bad had happened because there was every indication that it had. If that wasn't bad enough, he had felt shame, because he could tell that Beth had been scared of him. She had tried to conceal it, but she had been genuinely scared of him for the first time since he'd known her, and that bothered him to no end.

Good or bad, Jack had wanted to know what had happened. He hadn't wanted Beth looking at him like that anymore, and the sooner he could find an innocent reason for the blood, he had figured, the sooner she'd go back to looking at him like she had used to. He had just prayed, literally prayed to God, that it wasn't as bad as he suspected it was. But it had been.

They hadn't had to wait long to find out. Todd and Ron had started calling within an hour of Jack and Beth waking up. The cops had been looking for Jack, and they were asking about those bikers. That was all they had known, but they had known from the officers' demeanor that Jack needed to leave town if he didn't want to spend a great deal of his near future in a jail cell. Of course, they had covered for him. Ron and Todd had told the officers Jack had taken off the night before, and they had no idea where he was.

Ron and Todd would lie to the cops for Jack; that

had never been in question. But it wouldn't take the cops long to track Jack down all the same. Plenty of other people had known Jack was with Beth, most of whom wouldn't be shy about pointing the cops in the right direction. Despite the ridiculous stories he'd told many at the party of where he was going, he'd told more than a few of his regular buyers over that past week that he was moving in with his girlfriend Beth who worked at Western State. Jack had figured a hard knock on the door could happen any time They had sacked all the bloody sheets and clothes before remaking the bed and taking showers. Jack and Beth hadn't spoken as they worked, they had just jointly and intuitively carried out their tasks. Cleaning up had taken them ten silent minutes.

Pondering any decision for too long was poison to Jack. It was just like that, like the pondering really was poison. His stomach made terrible sounds, like the creaking a sinking ship makes when water pressure begins to implode it. His head throbbed. He shook all over. He sweated buckets and buckets and buckets. It was the anticipation he couldn't handle. Jack had no avoidance mechanism, and no ability to stop his ruminations. He always felt as though anything that *might* happen was currently happening to him. Making a decision, and taking physical steps to ensure he couldn't change his mind later, gave him certainty and alleviated the illness of pondering. Even when the decision turned out to be stupid or impulsive, he felt better. In reality, it was just his OCD compelling him to seek certainty about a situation that he did not accept and could not control, and those assurances that were bought through rash actions were always fleeting.

It had seemed clear to Jack that either running or staying meant being separated from Beth, but that staying and dealing with whatever happened meant that he might have a chance to be with her someday. Running would likely have meant leaving her for good. After his shower, he had asked her to go away with him for a few days. Packing some clothes had taken five more minutes, and with that, they were off.

Traveling and traveling, more driving to places that didn't even matter. It had seemed to Jack this was the totality of his life, even though Jack really didn't go that many places. "How can somebody spend as much time travelin' as I do, and still go nowhere interestin'?" He'd go places to get to things, and to get away from things and people, but no place ever sufficed. On that day they had traveled in Beth's Volkswagen Jetta. Everybody had owned a Volkswagen in the nineties. Nobody had driven anything else. Jack had thought, when he got back from wherever they were going to send him that time, that he was going to get himself a Volkswagen; not a Volvo, a Volkswagen. He had arrived back in Tacoma, and a little vacation was all Jack had needed to get his head straight about what he had to do next. His life had been about to hit the skids again when it had never really gotten off them from the last time. He had laughed to himself. "I fuckin' suppose 'the skids' are a multileveled journey. Man, what I wouldn't give to just be on the skids that I'd just been on a few days ago instead of the fucked-up skids I'm on now." Jack still hadn't even known what the new skids were, since he still hadn't known what had happened the night before. He had just known the present skids were worse than the previous ones.

Instead of a lifetime with Beth, he'd gotten three days in Long Beach Washington.

Beth had said, "What do you want to do first?"

"Find a time machine. If we go back about thirty-six hours, that ought to do it," had been Jack's response.

"Seriously! Your negative sarcasm is pretty funny when there's nothing at stake. Right now, it's less funny, and more desperate. Desperate isn't a good look on you, so if you're going be funny like that, be funny about something that's worth laughing about. Okay?"

Jack had felt like an asshole. She had been sweet and acted positive about a situation that negatively affected her, too, a situation that scared her and that she had done nothing to bring on herself. Meanwhile, Jack had sulked during what was likely to be the last days they'd spend together, at least for a while. He knew he'd had no right to. His actions, whatever they turned out to be, had caused the situation.

"How 'bout the motel," had been Jack's tardy response to the initial question.

It was funny how people appeared to you in everyday life, and at certain times became other people. They literally became different people—not different personality traits, but entirely different people. On many occasions, Jack became a different person. It happened when he was drunk and high, or in the ugly depths of one of his many mental illnesses.

Sometimes he was taller. Sometimes his eyes would change color and shape. His whole face, his whole complexion, would change. His voice, tone, inflection, vernacular—they'd change. Just like he was a different person altogether. The change in his body language was especially eerie. In order to notice the changes to his voice, eyes, shape of his mouth, or complexion, you had to be close to him.

His radically different body language and unexplained drastic height gain were noticeable from afar. Body language and height didn't change; they were hardwired. Mannerisms came out whether you liked it or not. In poker, it was called a tell. Body language let people know who was coming. The hand signals, posture, and facial twitches were huge neon signs as big as the ones on the Vegas strip telling all that were paying attention who was showing up in that body. Law enforcement agencies used them to identify people. It must have been some primitive safety mechanism protecting him. It was urban camouflage. It was effective, and he probably never even knew he had it.

Maybe it was possession. Maybe there was really somebody else residing inside certain people's bodies, or perhaps spirits just stopped by to visit the city and utilize bodies with personalities that were vacant enough for them to slide into unnoticed. A spirit periodically inhabiting Jack would have explained a lot, but more likely it was just urban camouflage. It was just one more of those latent Darwinian advantages buried in Jack that he had never learned how to utilize, but that had served to keep him alive nonetheless.

That different person syndrome happened mostly in times of extreme emotion. Jack never seemed to notice it in himself, but he had noticed it in Beth when he was fucking her. Jack had never fucked the Beth that he knew from the hospital. The nurse. That was the Beth he loved, but she had never showed up for sex. The other girl had always showed up. That other girl had been the one with the jet-black hair that reflected light the way skyscraper windows did when the sun hit them in the middle of the day, so black it was blue like a Crow feather. That one's face had been sharper, more carved, with pointed features. The straight, narrow nose had become more like a ski-jump. The cheeks had been raised in an impossibly high and unnatural fashion. The chin had pulled the same trick, only in a downward motion, while the normally soft shade of her pink skin had turned ivory. Her body had turned stiff and rigid, not supple like nurse Beth's body.

All in all, the appearance of this more intense-looking individual had rattled Jack quite a bit at first, and one time in the hospital he had asked her about her shocking transformation. The look in her darkening eyes, eyes that reminded Jack of huge pools of spent motor oil, had told him what he needed to know without her even moving the sharp, dark lips that were not her own. With body language that was also not her own, and a deep voice that resembled her sweet mousy one but little, she had attempted to explain Jack's reaction but had succeeded only in piquing his interest in this most strange of human phenomena. The fact that she had turned into the other girl while she explained it to him had scared Jack quite a bit.

That other sharp Beth had told Jack:

"You see, it's probably just your perception of me that's changed because of the strange circumstance that we've found ourselves in. You're just seeing me differently based on the highly emotional state that sex brings on. Sometimes, you appear to be another person, too. Have you ever met yourself in a mental episode, or during a bender? That's all it is. We're all somebody else sometimes."

Jack hadn't understood her, but he had nodded as though he had. "She was fuckin' right 'bout somethin'. I was seein' her differently, but it was because she'd taken a back seat in her own body, not because of the BS that doppelganger spun at me. She wasn't the one in charge, but she was there. Sometimes it used to feel like cheatin' to me, but after while it just felt like a threesome. Maybe sometimes when I'm loaded it's a foursome. Maybe sometimes it's two total strangers using our bodies to have indiscriminate sex. Who fuckin' knows."

In Washington State, just because the beach was right outside didn't mean you wanted to go there every day. Washingtonians understood this. To people in Washington, the beach was only a semi-event. Not all coastal areas were white sand and blue water. Here, it was clouds and rain most of the year. In southern California, the beach was nice year-round.

The beaches looked different around there. There were rocks and driftwood everywhere. Crusty clumps of sand crunched under your feet like dirt clods, and waves of ice-cold green water battered those hard beaches all day long. Seaweed washed up during low tide. It looked like some giant drying his homemade green spinach pasta on the beach. Algae-covered rocks that looked like sea monsters dotted the landscape and were serious trip hazards.

Even in the summer, when it was nice there, Washington beaches were a hard sell. In LA, the sand was white, and the water was that fake-ass aqua blue you saw in colored contact lenses. You half expected Pam Anderson to come running down the beach with her flotation devices bouncing in slow motion.

Running barefoot on the beach in Washington was more likely to result in slipping on a dead crab or cutting your foot on a broken seashell, than a lifeguard in a bathing suit rushing to your aid. As a matter of fact, the lifeguard presence at most Washington beaches was pretty sparse. But if you drowned, there would certainly be some volunteer firefighters from the local station waiting for your body to wash up at high tide. "Washington's coast is actually a couple hours' drive from the big cities in the Puget Sound, so Bobby and Jim from the local volunteer fire station is most likely who you're puttin' your life in the hands of if somethin' goes wrong on your visit to a Washington beach. Good luck with that, you fucker tourists."

Jack and Beth had spent three days at Long Beach sleeping in a motel room that he hadn't been able to remember the décor of a month later. They had eaten meals that he hadn't tasted. They had walked on the town's boardwalk, but Jack hardly remembered arriving or leaving the town at all. Morning had been afternoon, and afternoon had, in turn, become bedtime at blinding speed. A few times, Jack had forgotten about his situation, but only for a few minutes here and there. Jack's mind had refused to allow him to be present, and as such, the three days with Beth at the beach had felt like three hours at best, and while he hadn't known it yet, a three-year sentence awaited him.

Afterword

I can't say where you came across this book, but my best guess would be that you found it in a box of castoff garbage by the curb outside the cheap apartment complex at the end of your road. That guy that lived in the noisy apartment was just evicted, and this little novella was just some superfluous stack of somewhat uninformative paper disguised as a book by a cheap book binding and publishing house logo. Trust me, even the publishing house logo is a smoke show, just my plausible camouflage for a self-publishing operation consisting of me, and me alone, a one-man band.

As you might have already guessed from the title, this is the second part of a story. Specifically, it's the middle of Jack's story. He's a guy that consistently failed to clear a bar so low he could have tripped over it. Jacks are all over the world. Most of you know a Jack. I've known several. I've even been a Jack in the past. I spend a lot of time and effort these days doing my best not to turn back into a

Jack, but I digress. That noisy guy from the recently vacated apartment is definitely a Jack. He's not a bad guy. He's actually a pretty fun guy under the right set of circumstances. Anyway, there are two more novellas, and Jack has got a lot more story to tell, but you might want to keep diggin' in the the box of garbarge to see if Mr. Evicted had Sleeping in the Daytime. That's the first novella. He probably didn't, but hey keep lookin.' You never know.

Next up is *Squatting in the Shadow of an Ant*, and Jack does his best to conceal himself withing that tiny shadow. If you dig through enough dumpsters, you might find a copy of that too. If not, your best bet is probably the free book rack outside the Powell's in downtown Portland. Hey, at least it won't cost you any money!

About the Author

I was a homeless teenager. Now I own a home. I was a high school dropout. Now I'm an attorney. I was an alcoholic. Now I'm sober. I was a kid well into adulthood. Now I'm the adult parent of kids. I was alone. Now I have people. I was a punk rock teenager. Now I'm a punk rock middleager. I was Jack. Now I'm Chris.

Thank you for reading Courting Mediocrity. I hope you enjoyed it. Reviews are the single most important factor to the success or failure of a book. Please take a moment and leave a short review at one, or preferably both, of the links below. Also please connect with me on social media, and join my email list for freebies.

Connect with Me and Subscribe to the Email List

https://blandcoffeepublishing.com

Also by Christopher J. Stockwell

If you love slummin' it in the PNW, check out the rest of the down and out series, my first gritty novel *The Antagonist's Handbook*, and the two books of the *City Attorney's Office* series. If you don't feel icky afterward, we'll refund your money.

A Lack of Intradimensional Sync

Jon is everywhere an nowhere. He slips out of himself and rides the infinite roads of existence itself. But infinite time is eventually infinite torment for a human brain that never asked for anything more than normality. Expected Release 2026.

Sleeping in the Daytime

The keystone of the down and out books, a first glance at Jack. He's the car wreck you can't take your eyes off. Sleeping in the Daytime lets you see him before serious deterioration has set in. Get ready, living like Jack is a full-time job.

Squatting in the Shadow of an Ant

Prisons, institutions, and punk houses! See how Jack winds up. Is that a light at the end of the tunnel? Yes, it is a car intent on running poor Jack down.

The Complete Down and Out in Seattle and Tacoma Series.

The three novellas of the Down and Out in Seattle and Tacoma Series in one volume. The down and out novellas are like coke, alcohol, and cigarettes. You can enjoy them separately, but they were meant to be consumed together.

City Attorney's Office: Book One, ProfessionalCamouflage

This first of a series of short romance novels is nothing more than a thinly-veiled disguise for a social and political satire piece. Is is dark humor, literary existential bullshit, a boring workplace romance. I don't fuckin' know, and I wrote the book.

City Attorney's Office Book Two: The Land of Lollipops and Suckers

This second, and last (?) of the City Attorney's Office books. People always ask me if a lawyer's life is like Law & Order or the Good Wife. It's neither, it's mostly like Matlock and Perry Mason having a beer with Saul Goodman. Enjoy!

The Complete City Attorney's Office Series

If you liked the love triangle between Ben, Maria, and Erin, you'll get closure. If you liked that fact that Ben is a monkey wrench dismantling the necessary cogs of justice, it's in there as well. If you just want the series to be over, so do it. Your welcome!

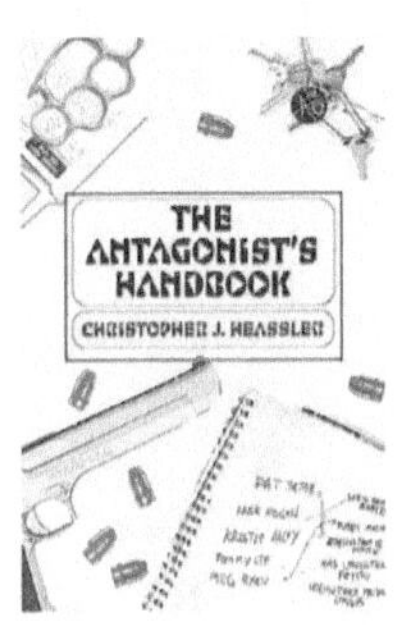

The Antagonist's Handbook

Stockwell's first novel, written under the pseudonym Christopher J. Heassler details the emergence of a paparazzi gang who exploit celebrities. The Antagonist's Handbook has long been out of print, but is scheduled for re-release in 2026.

www.ingramcontent.com/pod-product-compliance
Lightning Source LLC
Chambersburg PA
CBHW031054310726

48969CB00007B/2270